REFLEC

John Russ

When artist Clive H
Chief Inspector Ca
Yard is called upo
disappearance, and
lead him to question
Elsa Farraday. Elsa
has murdered the ar
liar manner puzzle
hesitates to make
larly as Hexley's bo
It is not until Calthorp calls in Dr.
Adam Castle, the psychiatrist investigator, that the strange mystery of Elsa's
behaviour and the artist's disappearance is solved.

ONE TO JUMP

George Douglas

When Detective Sergeant Dick Garrett spends his leave in Wellesbourne Green to persuade ex-crook Molly Bilton to marry him, he is faced with a mystery. Ace criminal Flint, previously known to Molly, is found dead with no clues to the killer. An assault on Gypsy Ben Thompson's daughter leads Garrett to risk his future in the Force. He suspects that one of the local police could be involved working hand in glove with the dead man.

Dedicated to
ARNOLD WALL

Power tends to corrupt, and
absolute power corrupts
absolutely. Great men are almost
always bad men.
LORD ACTON 1834–1902.

ROGER BAY

DEADLY
JIGSAW

Complete and Unabridged

LINFORD
Leicester

First published in Great Britain by
Robert Hale Limited
London

First Linford Edition
published 2006
by arrangement with
Robert Hale Limited
London

British Library CIP Data

Bay, Roger
    Deadly jigsaw.—Large print ed.—
Linford mystery library
    1. Detective and mystery stories
    2. Large type books
    I. Title
    823.9′14 [F]

    ISBN 1–84617–187–3

Published by
F. A. Thorpe (Publishing)
Anstey, Leicestershire

Set by Words & Graphics Ltd.
Anstey, Leicestershire
Printed and bound in Great Britain by
T. J. International Ltd., Padstow, Cornwall

This book is printed on acid-free paper

DEADLY JIGSAW

Fighting his way out of the closing net is Adam Kane, chief investigator for a large Insurance Company in Australia . . . Hot on the trail of a million dollar swindle Kane comes up against the Big Boy, a master criminal, and two of his deadly killers . . . The chase, with Kane being the hunted instead of the hunter, moves swiftly from Australia to Fiji, then down to the hot thermal pools of New Zealand before the last piece of the jigsaw is put into place.

Contents

1

Something to Sell

Adam Kane, chief investigator for the West Pacific Insurance Company, put the papers he had been studying into his brown leather briefcase, zipped it up, then felt around for his seat belt and secured it with a deft movement. He turned and looked out of the plane window as the turbo-jet approached the outskirts of Brisbane.

Five minutes later, at twelve minutes to five, the afternoon's flight from Townsville landed at Brisbane's Doomben Park airport.

The attractive brunette at the City Rent-A-Car desk in the main terminus looked up from her account book as Kane approached the counter. She gave him a smile.

'Yes, sir? May I be of some assistance to you?' she asked.

'I hope so. My name's Kane. You should have a car for me.'

'Oh, yes, Mr. Kane,' she answered. 'We received your telegram. I'm afraid there's going to be a few minutes delay. The boys have taken the car into the garage to get the brakes adjusted. They told me it would only take ten minutes. Would you mind waiting?'

'Not at all,' Kane answered. 'I'm not in a hurry.'

He leant against the counter and looked around the terminus. Most of the passengers who had disembarked with him had already left aboard a bus bound for the heart of Brisbane. Apart from a few airport employees the place was practically deserted.

A few minutes later a man in white overalls came through the swing doors. He had a set of car keys in his hand. He dropped them on the counter and said: 'Number sixteen's ready now, Yvonne. See you!'

The girl waved her hand in acknowledgement, picked up the keys and placed them into Kane's open palm. 'There you are, Mr. Kane. You'll find the car right outside the doors. It's a dark blue Ford Falcon.'

Kane signed the Insurance papers and contract forms and pocketed the keys. He was about to leave when he suddenly asked: 'I guess I'm your last customer for today. Maybe you'd like a lift into town?'

The girl looked up and studied Kane, a guarded expression on her face. Then she smiled. 'Well, that would be nice of you, Mr. Kane. I usually drive one of our cars back to the garage but they're all out tonight. If you like I'll just close shop. It shouldn't take me long.'

'Right,' said Kane, moving over to a seat a little way off. 'I'll meet you here.' He sat down and picked up a magazine from off the table and began flicking through it.

At first glance Adam Kane was often taken to be in his early twenties, but on a closer look it could be seen that he was quite a few years older. His face was oval in shape with a jutting jaw that spelt determination. His dark hair was long and wavy and shiny and stayed in place without the use of oils or preparations. His clothes were always immaculate and fitted fashionably to his lithe, well proportioned body. Adam Kane was 32 years of age, a bachelor and an opportunist.

It was this latter attribute which had made him talk to the girl. He had seen her on his way through the airport three days before. He had noticed that she wore no rings on her left hand, that she was attractive, and above all, looked intelligent. And it was usual for him, when meeting a girl with those three endowments, to at least try for a date. So far his plan was working smoothly.

A few minutes later the girl emerged from the office. She locked it behind her and walked over to where Kane was sitting. She was still wearing her firm's pale blue light-weight uniform but had changed from comfortable working shoes to a pair of high-heels.

Kane rose, quickly glancing her over. He approved of her sun-tanned legs and the way she walked. He also caught a hint of the exquisite perfume she was wearing.

Kane picked up his brief-case and escorted the girl out of the terminus. The dark blue Falcon was parked by the kerb and he opened the door for her. She slid across the front seat.

He drove slowly past the racecourse and then turned left towards the river. 'My name's Adam. Adam Kane. Your name's Yvonne, isn't it?' he asked. 'I overheard the man who brought in the keys talking to you.'

'Yes, Yvonne Morrison. It's funny, you're about the only person I've met who can pronounce my name properly.'

Kane laughed. He said: 'In my game that's one of the first things you learn.'

'What do you do, Adam?' she asked.

'I'm in the Insurance business. I work on the Investigation side. Checking claims and sorting the duds from the genuine.'

'Sounds exciting,' Yvonne said, turning and smiling up at him.

'Sometimes. It has its ups and downs.'

Kane was silent for a while. They were driving through the outskirts of Brisbane. Then he said: 'I'm staying at the Berkeley in the centre of town. If you have nothing planned for tonight perhaps you'd like to come and have dinner with me and then maybe a show or something.'

Yvonne looked out of the window for a few seconds. 'Yes, I'd like that very much. Thank you,' she replied softly.

'Good,' said Kane, bringing the Falcon to a stop at a red light. 'I'll pick you up at half seven. Whereabouts do you live from here?'

'Straight up this street,' Yvonne replied. 'I have a flat in a new block at the top.'

Kane followed Yvonne's directions and pulled to a halt in front of a block of brick-built flats. He opened the door for her and watched as she climbed the steps and went through the entrance way. She turned and waved to him before entering the elevator.

A smile spread across Kane's face as he executed a U-turn and headed towards the Berkeley. Then he started whistling. He chose a melody entitled: '*You Never Know!*'

He parked the Falcon in the parking area in front of his hotel, grabbed his brief-case from the back seat and then went up the steps. The girl at the desk smiled at him and said: 'Welcome back, Mr. Kane. We've all been wondering where you've been.'

'You should know me better than that by now, Carol,' said Kane. 'You know I don't let my left hand know what my right hand's going to do half the time.'

The receptionist smiled and handed him the key to his suite. She said: 'I had the laundry give your wardrobe a go over this morning. All your shirts have been cleaned and your suits pressed.'

'Thanks, Carol,' said Kane. 'I appreciate how you look after me.'

'Well, somebody has to,' she replied, a slight blush rising up her neck. 'Oh, yes. A man has been trying to contact you. He says it's urgent. I told him you weren't arriving until late. If he rings again shall I put him through?'

Kane nodded his head. 'He didn't leave his name?'

'No, but he had a slight stutter, if that's any help.'

Kane snapped his fingers. It was Danny Hurst. 'I know who it is. Yes, put him through if he calls again.' He turned and walked across the foyer to the doors of the elevator.

Carol watched him. She silently wished that some day he'd really notice her more for her looks and shape than for the way she looked after his interests. Still, she thought, a girl can keep wishing an awful long time.

As the elevator doors closed Kane leant against the wall and lit a cigarette. He wondered what Danny Hurst wanted to tell him and how much he'd want for the information. He let the smoke trickle out of his nostrils and waited for the elevator to arrive at the third floor.

Danny Hurst was the type of small-time thug that is hated by both sides. He is tolerated and used by the successful criminals as a lackey: one who will do the errands, the dirty work. The police, on the other hand, prefer to let him run free for they know that at any time he can be picked up and gleaned of any tidbits of information which he might have picked up on his rounds. He is never trusted with information of any importance for both sides know that he would try and sell it as soon as he could get to the nearest phone box.

Kane had come into contact with Danny Hurst two years before. He had been working on a fire claim and had reasons to suspect that the flames had been deliberately started. After hours of questioning and getting nowhere he had come across Danny, who, for a few dollars, had supplied the missing link by which Kane could prove his case. It had been something Danny had overheard in a bar.

Since then Kane had used Danny's help periodically. Even when he hadn't any information to sell Kane had given him a few dollars just to keep him sweet. As a man, Danny was not only a bore but a time-waster. What he thought was important was often common knowledge and could have been found by reading the newspapers. But at times he had his use . . .

Kane opened the door to his suite and looked around. The windows were open and the last of the sun's rays were streaming through. There were fresh flowers in a vase on the coffee table.

He strode across the thick wall-to-wall carpet and opened the door to his bedroom. He thought that Carol must really be on the ball. Only she could have supervised the preparation of the suite down to putting his black silk pyjamas on the bed.

He went into the bathroom and turned on the shower and then returned to the bedroom to strip. He was just going through the communicating doorway with a towel wrapped around his waist, when the phone rang.

Kane cursed silently under his breath and switched off the shower. He walked across the room and answered the phone.

It was Carol. She said: 'Oh, Mr. Kane. There's a gentleman down here to see you. It's the same one who's been phoning you. Shall I send him up?'

Kane thought quickly. Time was running short. He made up his mind. 'Yes. Have him come up right away. Thank you, Carol.'

Two minutes later there was a timid

knock on the door. Kane opened it. He had put on an orange towelling bathrobe and slippers. Danny Hurst was standing on the scatter rug outside the door. He was holding a chequered cap in his hands. An ominous smile was on his face.

'Come in, Danny,' said Kane. 'From the look on your face you've got something important to sell me.'

Danny walked in and looked around, as if he were a prospective tenant. He walked past the settee and then turned and faced Kane. He tapped his forehead with his finger.

'W . . . What I've got in here is w . . . worth a fortune, Mr. Kane,' Danny started his sales pitch. 'This is the big one. And it affects your Company.'

'If it's the Huntingdon diamonds, Danny, you're wasting your time and mine. They were handed over to the police yesterday.'

'N . . . No. This is bigger than them. The information I've g . . . got can save your Company a million dollars.'

'Oh, yes!' replied Kane, lighting a cigarette. 'A million dollars?'

Danny nodded his head. 'Th . . . that's what I said. But it's going to cost you.'

'How much?' asked Kane.

'F . . . five hundred dollars.'

Kane screwed up his eyes and sucked his breath in through pursed lips. 'Five hundred?' he exclaimed.

Danny nodded his head again.

The ash off Kane's cigarette dropped to the floor. He was deep in thought. He was in two minds as to whether to throw Danny out but there was something in the man's eyes and composure that was different from his usual form. Maybe, Kane concluded, he had stumbled across something big for a change; something that he knew was dynamite. He decided to play.

'I can't agree to a figure until I've heard what you've got to say, Danny. I'll tell you what, though. You tell me what you know and I'll evaluate it and if it's really something then I'll pay good money. But five hundred, that's a lot of money!'

Danny Hurst sat down on the arm of the settee. He threw his cap on to the cushions. 'D . . . does a million to one shot and the Melbourne Cup mean anything t . . . t . . . to you?'

Kane walked over to the cocktail cabinet and stared at Danny in the reflection of the mirror which hung above it. A curious sensation passed up his spine for Danny had mentioned about a policy which had only been signed the week before and was known to a selected few. He turned. 'Go on,' he said.

'I thought you'd b . . . be interested,' Danny stuttered. 'The Big Boy's behind it. You've h . . . heard of him, haven't you?'

It was Kane's turn to nod his head. The Big Boy and the organisation he headed had caused Kane's Company a lot of worry and money over the last few years. The police had him on their Most Wanted List but had come no closer to cracking the tightly-knit gang and finding out the identity of its leader than they had when they first started their investigations. He was like a ghost; he was there but nobody could prove it. And everything the Big Boy touched turned to gold, usually with an

Insurance Company footing the bill . . .

'Go on, Danny,' repeated Kane.

'It's a l . . . long story, Mr. Kane,' Danny began, nodding his head when Kane held up a bottle of whisky. 'I'm working evenings at a place out on Bank Street opposite the church there. It's run as a l . . . l . . . legitimate business but that's a front. The organisation owns it.' He stopped talking to take hold of the glass Kane held out for him, took a sip and then continued 'I just sweep the floors and t . . . tidy around the place. Two nights ago I wanted to use the phone. I thought I was the only one there. I picked up an extension and there were two men talking. I listened to what they said.'

Kane walked over to the windows and pulled the cord to close the venetians. It was almost dark outside.

'Th . . . they were discussing a pamphlet which was being printed. I've got a proof copy of one here. It's g . . . going to be used in the swindle . . . '

'Let's have a look at it,' said Kane, seriously. He watched as Danny reached for his cap and extracted a piece of paper from out of the lining. He unfolded it carefully and then handed it to Kane.

Kane took it over to his desk and switched on the adjustable light, bending the head down so that the beam fell on the piece of paper. The headline read: 'Double Your Money! Yes — Double Your Money Today without the slightest chance of losing a Cent!' Beneath, in smaller type, was a sales pitch which had been written by an advertising expert. The pamphlet was a cinch to get money out of the unwary.

Kane read through it twice before returning it. He said: 'I don't get it, Danny. This pamphlet means nothing.'

'It will w . . . when I tell you the r . . . rest. Your Company has signed a policy with Cheyney's, the Sydney bookmaking firm, right?'

'That's correct,' Kane replied.

'Th . . . they're offering a m . . . million to one on somebody forecasting the first three horses past the post in this y . . . year's Melbourne Cup.'

'That again is correct. But, Danny,

there's a deadline. Each bet has to be placed, at a dollar a go, before a certain date. At that time there'll be over 75 horses in the field. When the race is actually run there's only 24 starters. The chances of forecasting the first three a month before the race would be, well, a chance in a million!'

Danny laughed. He said: 'No, no. You don't get it. Look, I h . . . heard the whole plan. They said there were over 400,000 different variations but one of those would be the correct one.'

'That would be right,' said Kane, lighting another cigarette.

'S . . . o, the Big Boy and his organisation send out these pamphlets to every gambler throughout Australia offering to double their money. The s . . . suckers will flock to be in on it. The B . . . Big Boy will then cover those 400,000 odd chances with the money he gets back . . . '

'And win a million,' said Kane to himself. 'Jesus, you could be on to something here, Danny. And then he pays back the money plus . . . '

It was Danny's turn to interrupt. 'W . . . who said anything about paying the s . . . suckers back? The organisation would pocket the million dollars which y . . . your Company would have to pay out under the policy Cheyney's have taken out with them.'

Kane's body tingled with excitement. What he was hearing from Danny was, for once, dynamite. 'Who else have you told this story to?' asked Kane, suddenly.

Danny looked up at Kane. 'N . . . n . . . no one,' he said 'Only you.'

'Good. It wouldn't be too healthy if too many people knew about you hearing this conversation.'

'I k . . . know how to look after myself, Mr. Kane,' Danny replied.' W . . . well, what do you think? Do I get my f . . . five hundred?'

A special fund had been created by the West Pacific Insurance Company to deal with paying for information and informers and suchlike and Kane, being their top investigator, had full control over the fund. It was his to pay out as he thought fit, with no questions asked.

'Yes, Danny. You've earnt it this time,' said Kane, stubbing out his cigarette in a coloured glass ashtray. 'I don't carry that amount around with me but I can let you have a hundred on account.'

'W . . . when would I get the rest?' asked Danny.

'Later on tonight, if you like. I could cash a cheque down at the desk.' He looked at his watch and saw that it was creeping around to seven. 'Look, I'll meet you some place at eleven. How about that? There could be a few questions I want to ask you by then.'

Danny watched Kane as he went into the bedroom and came out with his wallet. His eyes sparkled as he saw the notes being taken out, counted and then handed to him. He licked his lips. 'You k . . . know the Casablanca?' asked Danny, counting through the notes. 'It's a nightspot up the t . . . top of Queen Street. I'll be there at eleven.'

'Right,' said Kane. 'I'll see you there.' He showed Danny to the door.

* * *

18

At exactly half past seven, after a fast shave and shower, Kane was knocking on the door of Yvonne's flat. He heard a movement behind the door and then it opened. Yvonne called out: 'Come in and make yourself comfortable, Adam. I'm afraid I'm a few minutes late. You've caught me dressing.'

Kane pushed the door open and walked in.

'Pour yourself a drink,' Yvonne called out from the bedroom. 'You'll find everything in the cupboard in the kitchen. You can fix me one as well, if you like. A small Scotch.'

Kane walked into the kitchen and opened the cupboard. He picked up the bottle by its neck and took it over to the sideboard. He proceeded to pour out two drinks.

Yvonne came out of her bedroom wearing a tight-fitting, well-cut dress which accentuated the curves of her body to their best advantage. Her sun-tanned skin looked even browner against the grape-coloured material. Kane turned around. He let a slight whistle out from between his teeth.

Yvonne smiled and turned her back to him. 'Do me up, please, Adam,' she asked. 'I can't reach.'

Kane searched for the zipper. He slid it up gently and hooked up the little eyes and then kissed her on the nape of the neck.

She turned and fell into his arms. She murmured: 'Why don't we stay here? I could cook us a nice steak each.'

'Well, now, that's a good idea. It just so happens that I'm very partial to home cooking.' He kissed her on her upturned mouth. 'There's just one little problem. I've got to meet a business friend of mine around eleven at a club called the Casablanca.'

Yvonne looked at her wristwatch over his shoulder. She said: 'But that's not for ages.'

'True! True!' Kane replied.

2

'Last Day'

Danny Hurst went straight from Kane's suite at the Berkeley to the public bar of the nearest hotel. Once there he ordered a large beer and flourished one of the twenty dollar bills as payment. He drank the beer quickly and noisily and then asked for another. He left the change on the counter while he drank.

Soon he was surrounded by three acquaintances, for Danny Hurst was known to quite a few characters around Brisbane, and it wasn't long before he was having his back slapped and being called a great chap and the other fatuous remarks that dead-beats make to each other when one of their number has made a score.

The bar was crowded and many a group stared for a while at the noisy newcomers and wondered what was the cause of celebration. Others, hoping for a hand-out, stood on the fringe waiting to be invited to join them at the bar.

There was one person in the bar who knew Danny Hurst but didn't go near him. He stayed in the background, behind a thick post, watching Danny's every move in the reflection of a conveniently placed mirror.

This man was small and thin with long, greasy hair which kept falling over his ears. He had a sallow complexion and a series of huge blackheads above the back of his collar. He was chewing, between sips of his drink, on a matchstick. His name was Ben Collins.

Ben Collins was a member of the organisation run by the Big Boy. He was a member because he was handy with a knife and was ruthless to the extreme. If somebody interfered with the Big Boy's plans then Ben Collins was called in to fix him. If somebody didn't carry out an order or disobeyed an instruction then it was Ben who was sent around to jog that person into action.

To look at him one would never have

taken him to be a strong man, but four years in a Japanese Prisoner of War camp had taught Ben Collins that strength wasn't the only persuasive power; the glint of sharp steel worked just as well.

After half an hour Ben Collins noticed that the group were preparing to move out of the bar. He finished his drink quickly, threw away his chewed match, and waited for them to make the first move.

Why Ben Collins was concerning himself about the spending habits of Danny Hurst even Ben Collins couldn't have answered at that precise moment. He knew that Danny worked nights at the printing works; sweeping the floors, emptying the garbage cans and cleaning up the mess left by the printers, and he knew what he was paid for his troubles. He also knew of Danny's reputation as an informer and by putting two and two together he was wondering, at the back of his mind, whether this sudden spending spree had anything to do with the organisation's secrets.

He followed the four men outside and

saw them entering a cab. There was another one on the rank and Ben opened the door and climbed in, giving the driver his instructions to tail them. After ten minutes driving he knew where Danny Hurst and his friends were heading.

Trotting has a big following in Australia, and the night meetings attract great crowds. The track is oval in shape, five to six furlongs in length and floodlit. The horses, or trotters as they are called, pull a lightweight sulky behind them upon which the driver sits. The Trots are a great favourite with the gambling public for they really get their money's worth of excitement, especially if an outsider romps home or two sulkys touch wheels rounding the home turn.

Danny Hurst and his friends arrived at the track just after the start of the fourth race. They went straight to the bar and ordered a round of beers. While they drank Danny studied the programme which he had bought at the gate. He looked up the starters in the fifth race; a handicap event over a mile and a half.

There were twelve in the field. The

favourite, so one of his mates informed him, was the first horse on the card but Danny, after a quick run through the names, liked the sound of the sixth horse. It was called: LAST DAY.

'I fancy this one,' he said. 'I'm going t . . . to put ten dollars on its n . . . nose.'

The roar from the crowd in the grandstands rose as the trotters in the fourth race approached the post. Minutes later, once the places were verified, the bar began to fill up with disgruntled punters who tore up their tickets and threw them to the ground with disgust before ordering their drinks. Danny and his friends were jostled to the end of the bar.

Danny managed to catch the eye of one of the barmaids and he held up a two dollar note to indicate another round. When she had poured the beers and delivered them he handed her the note and told her to keep the change. The girl took the note with a flourish and smiled mechanically, but not with her eyes. Danny thought she looked tired.

'Keep an eye on my b . . . beer,' said

Danny, after two swallows. 'I'll see what kind of odds I can get.' He turned and wandered off in the direction of the bookmakers' stands.

This was the chance Ben Collins had been waiting for. He had been standing in the background, watching and waiting. Now he moved.

He walked up to the bar and took Danny Hurst's place before anyone else could get there. He leant one elbow on the bar and waved a five dollar note about in his hand. He turned his head and looked at the three men.

'Didn't I see you fellows in the pub up George Street about half an hour ago?' he asked. 'Yeah, it was you lot. You were with Danny. How's it going?'

'Not bad,' answered one.

'Yeah, so it seems. Danny was looking happy with life. What happened? Did his grandmother die and leave him a few?'

'Sort of,' the man answered. 'You know Danny?'

'Yeah, we're old mates. Who did he tickle this time?' asked Ben.

The man who had been talking to Ben

kept quiet but one of the other two spoke up. 'Joker from one of the Insurance Companies. Paid him a hundred on account. Danny's got another four to come.'

'Go on!' exclaimed Ben Collins. 'Must have been a hot tip to get that much.'

'I'll say. Something to do with a swindle on the Melbourne Cup. He heard something at the place where he works.'

Ben Collins caught the barmaid's eye and ordered a beer. As an afterthought he told her to refill the glasses of the three men standing to his left. ' . . . and bring a new one for my old friend Danny,' he called out.

Ben brought the glass to his lips, said 'Cheers', and sank the beer in one swallow. He turned and said: 'Well, must be getting back. Give my regards to Danny.' He waved his hand and disappeared into the crowd.

Danny Hurst returned to the bar with a smile on his face. He picked up his glass and drained it. 'G . . . got twenty to one on it,' he said, picking up the full glass which was pushed in front of him.

'Bloody thing must be lame. Who bought t . . . this one?'

'Mate of yours,' replied one of his drinking friends.

'Oh yeah! Come on, l . . . let's go and watch the old nag.'

They left the bar and wandered through the crowd to the grandstand. The long rows of wooden seats were full so they went down to the edge of the track and leant on the railings. The trotters were moving around to the mobile start.

Minutes later the field was in position and the crowd went quiet. The truck began moving down the track with the trotters and sulkies behind it. When it reached the starting post the truck accelerated along the track, its wing-like gates folding forward. It pulled up to a halt on the outside of the track while the field overtook it.

The commentator took over and named, in a voice which could only just be heard above the roar of the crowd, the position of the twelve horses. Danny could see that his was third from last.

The field thundered past the grand-stand, the flashing hooves flicking lumps of dirt high into the air. Danny's horse, LAST DAY, was on the outside at the back of the field. It had moved on one place.

'C . . . come on!' yelled Danny. 'Move your b . . . bloody self!'

LAST DAY held its position during the next circuit of the track. As they approached the winning post the bell rang, signalling the last lap. The crowd in the grandstand were on their feet. The noise was deafening.

Along the back straight LAST DAY picked up a couple of places and as they rounded the home turn, veered out so that it had a clear run at the post.

It was hard to see, as they approached the post, who was in the lead but as they careered past the grandstand, Danny noticed that his horse was in the first three. It was a tremendous finish.

'What do y . . . you reckon?' Danny asked, excitedly. 'Was it in f . . . front?'

Nobody could tell him for sure and even the judges had asked for a photo. It was that close.

The minutes ticked by with a curious calm covering the whole track. Then the lights flickered on the in-field board and the commentator named the winner. It was number six: LAST DAY, by a nose. The outsider had won!

'S . . . stone the bleeding crows!' was all that Danny could say as his mates slapped him on the back and led him through the milling crowd to the bookmaker's area.

Danny's eyes bulged with greed as the notes were counted into his hand. He folded them neatly and placed them in his back pocket. He led the way to the bar. 'What's it g . . . going to be, fellows?' he asked.

They all asked for whisky and Danny slapped a twenty dollar note on the bar top and shouted out the order. He was feeling on top of the world.

They were waiting for the second round to be served when Danny looked up and saw Ben Collins for the first time. He was leaning on the other end of the bar, facing them, a matchstick stuck in one corner of his mouth.

Danny quickly turned his head away, a cold shiver running down his back as he recognised the organisation's trouble-shooter.

'What's up, Danny?' asked one of his drinking friends. 'That fellow's one of your mates. He's the one who bought you that drink before the last race.'

'W . . . what do you mean, b . . . b . . . bought me a drink?'

They told him. Beads of perspiration broke out on Danny's forehead as he listened.

'Y . . . you told h . . . him that?' asked Danny, incredulously.

'Why not? You told us. He thought it was a bit of a giggle.'

Danny didn't answer. He snatched up the change on the bar top and headed off into the crowd.

Panic hits in various forms. With Danny there was a cold ache in his stomach while his legs turned to jelly. His brain wouldn't function. All he could tell himself was that his life was in danger. He ran blindly towards the exit.

An empty taxi happened to be pulling

into the rank outside the track and Danny wrenched the door open and jumped in. He waved a twenty dollar note in front of the driver's eyes and, stuttering badly, told him to drive into the city.

The driver shrugged his shoulders, rammed the gear lever into first and made a U-turn. He glanced at his passenger in the rearview mirror and saw that he was looking out of the back window.

'Where to, mate?' the driver asked.

'Q . . . Queen Street. Anywhere. Get m . . . moving!'

'Hold your water, mate! It can't be that urgent!'

Danny let out a sound which was close to a whimper. Sweat was running down his cheekbones. He wiped his chin with the back of his hand.

The taxi overtook several cars and then, with its headlights blazing, tore down a long straight stretch. Danny watched the traffic behind them. Just when they were nearing the end of the straight he saw the headlights of another car pull out and overtake the cars which they had passed several seconds before.

'F . . . faster! F . . . faster!' Danny yelled.

'Are you in some kind of trouble?' asked the driver, over his shoulder.

'W . . . where are we now?' asked Danny.

'Top end of Queen Street. You didn't answer . . . '

'Let me out! Stop!'

The driver slammed on the brakes. 'I can't change that twenty, mate. Have you got anything . . . '

Danny opened the car door and let himself out. He threw the twenty dollar note at the driver and ran to the nearest corner.

The driver picked up the note and shrugged his shoulders for the second time. He thought that taxi drivers, especially on the night shift, met some right royal Charley's. He pocketed the note and drove towards the nearest rank.

Another taxi appeared around the bend in the road before Danny made the safety of the corner. For a split second he was caught in the glare of the headlights. As he ran he heard the sound of a car door slamming.

Danny's breath came in labouring

gasps. The unaccustomed exertion was making itself felt. He stopped at a lamp post and took stock of his surroundings. The street he had entered was long and straight. It was also well lit. The buildings were mainly warehouses which offered him little protection.

Then he saw the alleyway. It was several yards further along the street. It ran between two high buildings. The entrance was in darkness. He started running towards it.

Ben Collins appeared around the corner just as Danny Hurst made the alleyway. He caught a glimpse of a moving figure just before it disappeared from sight. Ben smiled to himself. He was enjoying the chase. He took his knife out from its shoulder sheath and walked towards the shadow of darkness.

Danny ran blindly. He knew that he should never have opened his mouth about the money; that he should have kept quiet, but it was too late now. While he ran he tried to work out some kind of plan. If, he told himself, he could get to the Casablanca by eleven and meet Kane he could get the money and then high-tail it out of town. Even though he hadn't seen Ben Collins behind him, he knew that he was there. And knowing of Ben Collins's reputation made him run just that bit faster . . .

He reached the end of the alley and cursed as the street lighting made him stand out like a sore thumb. He turned to his left and ran blindly down the main street. Without looking at the traffic he crossed to the opposite corner, hid in a doorway and looked back to the entrance of the alleyway. Ben Collins had just emerged and Danny watched him as he looked up and down the street, hesitating which way to go. Then he saw him turn and walk in his direction.

A tram pulled to a halt in front of Danny, blocking Ben Collins from his view. He summed up the situation in a second. Here was his way out. He ran to the tram and climbed aboard.

Danny looked out of the window, shielding himself behind a passenger's newspaper when they passed the spot where he had last seen Collins. There was no sign of him.

The tram stopped at the next corner and several people got off. Danny made his way to the opposite side of the tram and looked out of the off-side exit, leaning over the safety bar which was wedged in place across the doorway. There was still no sign of Ben Collins.

Danny relaxed and turned around. He pulled out his grubby handkerchief and wiped the perspiration off his forehead.

And then he saw him! Ben Collins was on the tram making his way up the centre aisle towards him. He had his right hand inside his coat.

The tram was between stops and moving fast. There was only one way out for Danny and that was to jump off from the doorway where he was standing and get to hell out of town. He would have to contact Kane for the rest of the money at a later date.

Ben Collins was having a hard time getting past a tall, elderly man and Danny took that chance of getting off. He ducked underneath the safety rail and jumped off. Just as he let go of the doorway he saw his mistake. Another tram was approaching on the other track. He had jumped right into its path.

The driver switched on the brakes but there was nothing he could do. Danny's legs had gone under the grill and his body was pinned underneath one of the heavy wheels. Both trams ground to a halt.

Ben Collins had seen the accident. He smiled to himself, stepped off the tram and walked back up the road and stood on the outskirts of the crowd which had formed.

'Jumped off that tram there right into the path . . . ' screamed a woman.

' . . . bloody fool must've been drunk . . . ' said another.

'Look at the money on the road! It won't do him much good . . . '

'Is he dead?' someone asked Ben.

Ben walked over to make sure. He took one look at the mangled, twisted body. He thought that they didn't come any deader. He crossed the road and stood in a doorway, watching as the ambulance arrived. He was getting a kick out of the scene.

3

The Matchstick Man

A church clock was striking half after ten as Kane and Yvonne drove slowly down Queen Street looking for the side turning where the nightclub was situated.

They could see two trams and a crowd ahead and slowed down. A policeman signalled them past the accident. Just as the ambulance was reversing towards the still figure on the ground, the crowd moved back and Kane got a glimpse of the body. He didn't recognise it as being Danny Hurst.

Yvonne shuddered. 'How ghastly,' she said.

Kane concentrated on the road ahead. He patted her on the knee.

They found the turning where the nightclub was and Kane found a parking space and reversed the car into it. He held Yvonne's arm as they crossed the

38

road and went down the steps to the entrance.

A youth of about eighteen was sitting behind the desk in the brightly painted foyer of the club. He was reading a comic. Without looking up he tore off two tickets from a roll and pushed them across the top towards Kane.

Kane stared at the youth, his anger rising, but then decided it wasn't worth it. He took out his wallet, paid for the tickets and then escorted Yvonne through a doorway which was covered by a thick red velvet curtain.

A waiter pulled himself away from the wall where he was resting and approached them. He held his hand out for the tickets. Kane gave them to him with a scowl. He turned to Yvonne and said: 'Look, this place is already giving me the berries. I'm sorry, I should never have brought you here.'

'Please let's stay, Adam,' Yvonne replied, squeezing his arm. 'I'm quite enjoying it.'

The waiter showed them to a table in the far corner. Kane held Yvonne's chair while she sat down. He sat opposite her and took a quick look around the club.

The place was so badly illuminated that it took several seconds for his eyes to become adjusted. When at last he could see, he saw that the club consisted of a small polished dance area surrounded by table and chairs of the type they were sitting at. The place was two-thirds full with a clientele that could only be classed as hippies or dead-beats. The club wouldn't have rated a mention in any tourist brochure.

A five-piece band was playing a South American love song which sounded more like a Fijian War Chant, and two or three couples were attempting to dance to it.

The waiter, who had taken their tickets, sidled up to the table. He held a tattered and grease-stained menu in his hand.

'Would you like a drink while we're waiting?' Kane asked Yvonne, pushing the menu into the centre of the table with his finger tip.

'Yes, a Scotch, thanks,' she replied. Kane ordered two.

Soon after the drinks had arrived the

band stopped playing and the musicians put down their instruments. They left the rostrum through a dark curtain at the rear.

The lights went out suddenly throwing the club into semi-darkness. Then a spotlight flashed on and was directed at the centre dance area. From the loud-speakers came some hot recorded music.

They watched as a girl came dancing into the limelight. She was wearing a full length sequin-covered white evening dress which sparkled in the beam. She danced a few steps to the music and then started singing.

Yvonne looked into Kane's eyes and smiled. Kane shrugged his shoulders and put a resigned expression on his face. There was nothing they could do; they would have to sit through it.

The girl sang three numbers and one encore although it would have been hard to figure out who requested the encore for hardly anyone applauded her perfor-mance.

The coloured lights were switched on again when the floorshow was over and the band came back to the rostrum. One of them staggered up the steps. He was so drunk he could hardly stand. They picked up their instruments and attempted to play a Cuban love song.

Kane looked at his wristwatch. He saw that it was almost half after eleven. He looked slowly around the club for Danny Hurst. There was no sign of him.

'Is something worrying you, Adam?' Yvonne asked, when she saw the frown crease his forehead.

'No, not really. I was meant to meet a contact of mine here at eleven to give him some money. He's the type that's always on time when there's money in the offering.'

'Does he know where you're staying?' Yvonne asked. 'Perhaps he can't make it.'

'Yes,' replied Kane, slowly. 'He's most probably got tied up. There'll most probably be a message for me when I get back. Look, let's have another drink. If he doesn't turn up during the next half-hour, we'll call it a day.'

They sat, watching the dancers and listening to the band, until a few minutes after midnight. Then Kane decided it was time to leave. They got up from the table and made their way through the heavy velvet curtain.

Kane was silent as he drove Yvonne back to her apartment. He was concerned about Danny's non-appearance. He thought that the appointment at the Casablanca would have been one that Danny would definitely have made.

He took Yvonne up to her door but pleaded exhaustion when she invited him in for a cup of coffee. He kissed her goodbye on her upturned lips and then made his way back to the elevator.

Kane drove slowly back to the Berkeley. He left the car parked outside with the engine running and went up the steps and through the swing doors. He approached the night porter's desk and asked if there had been any messages for him. The night porter shook his head.

Kane returned to the car and sat, drumming his fingers on the steering wheel. After a minute he engaged the gears and drove quickly through the sleeping city.

Bank street was in the path of the proposed northern motorway. Many of the old buildings had already been torn down and demolished and the ones that were left standing were at the far end. Kane passed the parked bulldozers and graders as he drove slowly along the darkened street.

The old, derelict Church, which Danny had mentioned, loomed up in the beam of the headlights. A notice board, nailed across the bolted doors, bore the legend: 'CHURCH CLOSED — BUT JESUS STILL LOVES YOU'. Kane reversed the Falcon up the weed-encroached driveway and switched off the lights and engine. He sat staring at the building on the other side of the street.

The street lighting had been the first thing to go and the street was dark and full of shadows. The building looked strangely forbidding. It was surrounded by a low hedge and the small plot of land between the street and the front of the building was covered with tall, prickly-looking weeds and wind-sown scrub.

As Kane's eyes became adjusted he

began picking out details. The building was an old single-storied house. The front door area had been roughly rebuilt so that now there were two thick wooden doors reaching across the whole width of the wide veranda. These were locked from the outside by a large chain and equally large padlock. The windows were barred, with wire mesh on the outside and vertical bars inside.

Kane let himself out of the car and stood, facing the house. He took a narrow pen-shaped flashlight out from his inside coat pocket and a small bunch of keys from another. He walked silently across the street.

The windows at the back of the house were equally well protected but the back door, like most back doors, had been forgotten. It was held by a single spring-type lock.

Kane smiled to himself, switched on the flashlight pen and got working on the lock with his keys. It took him three minutes to find its secret.

The door still held even though the lock was open. Kane could feel, by pressing against it, that it was bolted from the inside. He cursed and went back to the double front doors.

The new, heavy brass padlock presented a bit of a problem but eventually yielded to Kane's seemingly magic touch. The chain slipped out of his hand as he opened the lock and clanged against the heavy doors. Kane froze and looked about him. There was no other sound in the dark street.

There was hardly any ventilation and the inside of the building was hot and stuffy. The smell of printer's ink and well-oiled machinery filtered into his nostrils as he let himself through the door.

Kane closed the door as best he could and then swung the narrow beam of the torch around the interior. To his right was a glass doorway and a large plate-glass window. Behind them, he could see, was an office of sorts. A desk and swivel chair were set in one corner of it and behind them a set of grey steel filing cabinets. The floor space was littered with large, sealed cardboard boxes piled three high.

The door was locked.

Kane walked through into the factory part of the building. His beam picked out the machinery looking out of place amongst the littered floor and cluttered benches. Lead bars, for the linotype machines, were stacked two feet high in one corner. It was obvious to Kane that Danny Hurst hadn't been to work that night for the wastepaper baskets were full and scrap paper was lying everywhere.

The search began, even though Kane didn't know what he was looking for. He pulled out drawers and read every line of type he could find. He even read through the scraps of paper thrown into the wastepaper baskets. Eventually he had worked his way completely around the works without finding a thing that connected the printing works with being a cover for the Big Boy and his organisation. Everything he had seen and read pointed to the place being a legitimate business concern.

Kane studied the office door. The lock was a Yale and he had it fixed within seconds. The door made a creaking noise as he opened it.

There was only just enough room for him to squeeze by the cardboard boxes as he entered, so closely had they been stacked to the door. Kane made his way to the desk and sat down and lit a cigarette. With the cigarette dangling from his lips he methodically worked his way through the drawers, studying each invoice and piece of paper as he came to them. Once more he drew a blank. There was nothing of any importance left around.

He stubbed out his cigarette in an ashtray on the desk when he had finished and then turned his attention to the filing cabinets behind him. Again there was nothing.

'That leaves the boxes,' Kane said to himself, getting up and moving around the desk.

They were square and heavy. There were no markings on the outside or an address label. Each box was sealed with a length of strong self-adhesive tape wrapped around the seams.

Kane picked up a chromium-plated letter opener and cut the black tape in a couple of places. He then tore the strip off and opened the flaps of the box backwards.

Stacked in bundles of at least two hundred were thousands of printed pamphlets. Kane twisted the elastic band holding the top bundle until it broke. He licked his fingers and took off the top one and held it under the beam from the torch.

The pamphlet Kane held in his hand had exactly the same wording as the one Danny Hurst had shown him a few hours earlier. The only difference was that the spelling mistakes had been corrected.

Here was the proof Kane needed. If the information Danny had given him was correct about a proposed swindle on the Melbourne Cup, and everything was beginning to point in that direction, then the printed pamphlets definitely tied in the house as being used as a cover for the organisation. It was the first concrete piece of fact that Kane had ever been able to unearth about the Big Boy. It was a great start!

Kane took about twenty of the pamphlets and folded them neatly. He put them into his coat pocket. It was while he was attempting to re-seal the box with the adhesive tape that he heard the first hint that he wasn't alone. He stopped what he was doing and stayed, crouched on the floor, listening.

The chain on the front door rattled slightly and then a floorboard creaked as weight was placed on it.

Kane switched off the flashlight and picked up a heavy glass ashtray from off the desk. He silently made his way to the door and crouched behind it. By looking though the crack he could just see the entrance to the house. The door was open and the chain was swinging to and fro. While he was looking at the chain a trouser leg suddenly blocked his vision.

'Mister,' a scared voice tried to snarl. 'I've got a .45 Luger pointed at the top of your head. Stand up and turn around.'

Kane let out a sigh. He had been too

slow. He stood up and turned around and faced the wall.

'Drop that ashtray and place your hands on the wall.'

Kane did as he was told. He let the ashtray drop on to the carpeted floor. He heard the glass door being pushed open behind him.

'Don't move. Stay as you are.'

The door opened wider until it touched his left heel. He could hear the man breathing close behind him. Kane waited until he stepped through the doorway.

When he did, Kane moved. He had placed his heel until it was touching the door and when the man was half-way through Kane kicked back with all the force he could muster.

The idea worked. The door caught the man's wrist with a sharp crack. Kane swung around and went for the Luger. For a split second the gun was pointing straight at his stomach but the sudden movement had caught the gunman out. By the time he pulled the trigger the Luger was pointing at the ground.

The roar of the .45 exploding in the

office deafened Kane and the acrid fumes of the cordite almost blinded him. He kept hold of the gunman's wrist and began twisting it until the Luger dropped to the ground. Then Kane spun the gunman around and lifted his knee into his groin. A gasp of breath whistled past his ear before the man's body hit the ground.

Kane leant against the glass door and wiped the sweat off his forehead. When he had recovered, he picked up the Luger and took out the magazine clip. He saw that it was fully packed and that there was one up the spout. Kane unloaded the gun, threw it into the wastepaper basket, then put the clip and spare bullet into his back pocket.

He turned the gunman, who was out cold, over with his left foot and switched on his flashlight. Kane almost laughed when he directed the beam at the gunman's face.

At a rough guess Kane placed his age at being a little over eighteen. He had long dark hair covering his neck and ears and a ferocious-looking moustache to match.

But the face behind the whiskers was young and painfully thin and unexperienced. Somebody, Kane thought, had left a boy behind to do a man's work.

Kane threaded the chain and secured the padlock behind him as he left the building. He walked quickly through the long grass and scrub until he made the street. He looked both ways, saw that the street was clear, and made his way to his parked car.

He was feeling pleased with his investigation. Danny Hurst had been right for a change. The information he had overheard had all the signs of being correct. Finding the pamphlets had confirmed in Kane's mind that a swindle was being planned. All that remained now for him to do was to prepare a report, deliver it to his Company and have the policy cancelled. It was as easy as that!

There was only one thing that Kane felt uneasy about and that was Danny's non-appearance at the nightclub . . .

Kane opened the car door and slid across the seat. He turned the key and started the motor. As he turned onto the street he took a last look at the building where the pamphlets had been printed. He thought that the derelict house would be a good place for the police to start their investigation once they had been informed of the Big Boy's plan.

It was as Kane was driving past the parked bulldozers and road-making equipment that he heard the movement from the back seat. Before he had a chance to think, a hand grasped him around the throat and the tip of a sharp knife was pressed into the back of his neck. A voice said: 'You must be Danny's wide-eared friend. Make one wrong move and you'll be meeting him quicker than you think.'

Kane took his foot off the accelerator and looked into the rearview mirror. Leaning over the back seat, holding a long, thin throwing knife in his hand, was one of the ugliest looking men he had seen for many a day. Clenched between the man's teeth was a matchstick.

4

'What the Hell!'

Adam Kane brought the Falcon to a stop at the red traffic light. The point of the knife was still held against his neck. He could feel a thin trickle of blood seeping under his collar from the cut the knife had made when they had gone over a broken culvert in the road.

'Turn to the right. Take the road out of town.'

Ben Collins saw that Kane was looking at him in the rearview mirror. He said: 'Take it easy, buster. I'm watching you like a hawk. Make one slight move and I'll have you right here.'

A shiver of fear crept up Kane's spine. The way the man handled the knife and the way he spoke marked him as a killer. He knew he would have to do something pretty desperate to get out of the jam he was in but as long as the knife was pressed where it was there was little room for movement.

'You must be the fellow our mutual friend Danny put the hard word on earlier today. It's a good thing I thought about checking the printing works after catching up with him. You might have got away. How much did you give Danny?'

'I don't know what you mean,' Kane replied.

'Come off it, friend. You'll be telling me next you were looking around the place because you were thinking of buying it. Who do you work for? An Insurance Company?'

Kane kept quiet. He was trying to think.

The knife jabbed into Kane's neck again causing him to flinch. In the same movement Ben Collins reached over with his free hand and took Kane's wallet out from his coat pocket. 'Answer me when I ask you a question, fellow, otherwise your neck will look like a pin cushion.'

Kane could hear the wallet being unzipped. There was a rustle of paper money and then the sound of his plastic-coated identification card being withdrawn.

The wallet was thrown back on to the front seat, followed by the card. 'Adam Kane, eh? Investigator for the West Pacific Insurance Company? Well, Kane, my old mate, you've picked on a tough one this time. I just hope you've taken out a Life policy with your firm because somebody's going to be able to collect on it in about ten minutes time.'

Kane managed to laugh. 'This isn't Chicago, you know. You can't go around killing people ad lib. There's an efficient police force . . . '

'Shut up, Kane. You're making me sick!' yelled Ben.

Another light was against them and Kane braked slowly to a stop. He looked both ways and saw that there was a police officer on a motor cycle parked up the side road. An idea came to him.

The lights changed to green and Kane put his foot down hard on the accelerator. As the car took off it peeled rubber for about ten yards.

'Steady, Kane! Steady!' said Ben,

leaning forward and hooking the knife under Kane's coat collar. 'I should hate to make a mess of that front seat.'

Kane slowed the car down. He moved the wheel a fraction so that the front wheels went over the centre white line. Gradually he pulled back until he was almost on the kerb. He took a quick peek in the mirror. His idea hadn't worked. There was no sign of the police officer following them.

'Keep going along this road until I tell you to pull up,' said Ben, settling back into the seat. 'Don't forget that my knife's only two inches away from your jugular so don't try anything funny.'

Kane switched the headlights on to full beam as they approached the outskirts of Brisbane. He continued weaving the car towards the centre line and then back to the kerb.

'How did Pinky shape up?' asked Ben, spitting out the matchstick on to the floor of the car.

'Pinky?'

'The young fellow I sent in to get you. Did you finish him off? I heard a shot.'

Kane shook his head. 'No,' he replied. 'I just winded him a bit.'

Ben Collins shook his head slowly from side to side. 'Yeah, he's got a lot to learn, that fellow has. Wants to be a top hood but just between you and me I don't think he's got the makings. He hasn't got that killer instinct, if you know what I mean.'

'Like you?'

'That's right. Like me. Take tonight, for example. I'm getting a kick out of all this running around. Your friend Danny thought he could out-run me but his effort was pitiful. Silly bastard jumped off a tram going up Queen Street right into the path of an oncoming one. He died nice and quick. Suited me, really, because it looked like an accident. The Big Boy will be pleased when I tell him about it.'

'Who's this Big Boy of yours?' asked Kane. 'I'd like to know. He and his organisation has been causing my Company a lot of trouble these last few years.'

Ben Collins laughed. He said: 'You'll never find out, Kane. He's smart, real smart. I could tell you for all the good it would do you, though.'

'Well, why don't you? Or perhaps you're not big enough in the organisation to be trusted with a secret like that.'

'Shut your mouth, Kane. You don't know what you're talking about.' Ben Collins's face coloured slightly and he leant forward and dug the knife point into Kane's collar again. 'For that you're going to die just that little bit slower.'

Kane looked up into the rearview mirror to see if there was a chance of making a break for it. He saw that the gangster was putting another matchstick into his mouth.

It was while he was watching that he noticed a single headlight following them. His heart skipped a beat. About three hundred yards back was a motor cycle. He began to increase his speed.

'Killing me is not going to do you much good, you know that, don't you?' said Kane.

'And why's that?'

'Maybe I've already notified my Company about what I've found out.'

'I'll take a chance on that you haven't.

I'll tell you why. Danny Hurst has a reputation for being unreliable and a good investigator, like yourself, would want to check his story out first before putting in a report.'

'That's true,' said Kane. 'But directly I found those pamphlets tonight at that house I put through a phone call to my superior. Even if you manage to kill me the policy will be cancelled.'

'You put a phone call through from the place where Pinky jumped you?' asked Ben.

'That's right. And how do you . . . '

'You're a liar, Kane. A stupid liar. That phone was cut off yesterday morning. The Post Office boys took all the poles and wires down. They were in the way of the bulldozers.' Ben Collins laughed. He continued: 'You'll find it hard to pull a trick like that on me. My name's Ben Collins, not Danny Hurst.'

Kane swore under his breath. He felt crestfallen. His bluff, his bargaining bluff, hadn't worked. He looked up into the rearview mirror again.

The motor cyclist was catching them

up even though they were doing seventy. The gap between them was just over fifty yards. But Kane couldn't see whether it was the police officer or a civilian.

'Slow down and take the next turning to your left,' said Ben. 'I might as well get this job over and done with. You're beginning to bore me.'

'You don't honestly think you can get away with this, do you?' asked Kane, suddenly finding that his hands were shaking on the steering wheel.

'Who's going to stop me?' was all that Ben Collins replied.

Kane slowed down. He could feel beads of sweat forming on his forehead. He switched on the left hand indicator light. At almost the same second he heard a siren start up behind them.

'What the hell?' Ben Collins cried out, turning around to look out of the back window.

Kane slammed on the brakes and brought the Falcon to a screeching halt. He slewed the wheel around so that the car almost ran into the ditch, then opened the car door and threw himself on to the grass verge as the engine stalled.

The sound of the back door opening made Kane get to his feet and look around. He caught a quick glimpse of Ben Collins pushing his way through the hedge and then running towards a small wood which lay just off the road. He stood erect and got out his handkerchief and wiped the sweat from off his forehead. It had been close; too close!

'Okay, mister. What's going on here?'

Kane looked at the policeman. The man was standing a few feet away and had his hands on his hips. He looked as if he was expecting trouble.

'Officer, you may not know it but you have just saved my life,' said Kane.

'From the way you were driving you can say that again,' replied the policeman. 'Now come here and blow up this little plastic bag for me.'

Kane looked in the direction of the wood. He could just make out the form of Ben Collins dashing into the cover of trees. 'I'm not drunk and I'm not driving under the influence of drugs,' said Kane. 'I was driving like that so I'd attract your attention. I pulled away from some lights back further squealing the tyres so that you'd follow me.'

'You want me to believe that?' asked the policeman. 'If you wanted to attract my attention why didn't you pull up and talk to me? Anyhow, who was that person who ran away just now?'

'That was a hitch-hiker I was giving a lift to,' lied Kane. 'He had a knife to my throat and was threatening to kill me. Look, here's the marks. The only way I could get your attention was to drive carelessly and hope you'd pull me up.'

The policeman looked puzzled. He glanced over to the wood where Ben Collins had run to. He was undecided.

'Look,' said Kane. 'You can see I'm not drunk. How about escorting me back to Brisbane where I can give you a statement?'

'You're not drunk, I can see that from here. Wait a minute. I'm going to radio for a car. I don't know whether you're pulling my leg or something.'

'Suit yourself.' Kane thought he was giving the policeman a hard time, but it was the only way he could play things until he had time to think out his next move. He looked at his watch and saw that it was almost half after two.

Kane leant against the side of the car after retrieving his wallet and identification card. He drew slowly on a cigarette. He thought the best thing to do would be to get back into Brisbane, make a statement to the police along the lines of the hitch-hiker threatening him and then get back to the Berkeley. From there he'd be able to ring up the General Manager of his Company, Paul Smithers, and tell him the facts as he knew them. That way, Kane thought, there'd be somebody else in the know should anything unforeseen happen again.

A car, with its headlights blazing, came over the crest of the next hill. It was a police car. Kane thought that the roads must be crawling with them. This one had been less than two minutes away.

The police car and the motor cyclist followed behind Kane as they drove back to Brisbane. They reached the station and went into one of the small offices. Kane

65

was shown a seat and then an Inspector came in. He looked at Kane, recognised him and said: 'Why, hallo, Kane. What the hell have you been up to?'

Kane told him the story he had decided to stick to. He thought that to elaborate about the Melbourne Cup swindle, Danny Hurst's death and his meeting with Ben Collins could slow him down. He explained his erratic driving as a means to attract the attention of the police motor cyclist.

Inspector Barton made notes on a pad then looked up. He asked: 'I don't suppose you could describe this man, could you, Kane?'

'I'm sorry, Ken. It was dark and I only got a quick look at him,' lied Kane. 'My hazy description wouldn't help you too much.'

'I see,' Inspector Barton said, putting his pad and pencil down on the table. 'We'll make some inquiries, of course, but I can't promise anything. We seem to be plagued by this type of thing just lately. My advice is not to stop for anyone on the roads at night. Perhaps you've learnt a lesson.'

'You can say that again,' said Kane. 'Am I free to go now? I could do with a shower and then some sleep.'

'Surely,' said the Inspector. 'I'll show you out. We must get together for a drink sometime.'

Kane drove back to the Berkeley. He thought that to have told the true story of what had happened to him that night would have entailed a lot of explaining and that was one thing he didn't have time for. Maybe, at a later date, he'd be able to tell the whole story to Ken Barton over a pot of beer. Right now, though, he had work, important work to do.

He reached the Berkeley and went up to his suite and locked the door. He had a quick shower, stuck a piece of sticking plaster over the most serious of the knife pricks and then sat down on his bed and picked up the phone. He dialled the home number of the General Manager of the West Pacific Insurance Company: Paul Smithers.

The phone rang six times before the receiver at the other end was lifted, then a gruff voice asked: 'Yes, what is it?'

'Paul? This is Adam Kane. I've got something important to tell you and I'm afraid it can't wait until morning. There's just the faintest chance I won't be around. There's somebody gunning for me. He's already had one go.'

'Kane, what are you talking about?' The voice was now fully awake.

'It has something to do with a policy we've taken out with Cheyney's, the Sydney bookmaking firm, on their one million to one shot on the Melbourne Cup.'

'Right. Come around here right away. I'll get dressed and we can have a talk in the study. How soon can you make it?'

'I'll be there in half an hour,' Kane replied, replacing the receiver.

Just as Kane was about to leave his suite the phone rang. He had his hand on the door knob. He turned and looked at the white extension on the coffee table, then at his wristwatch. It showed ten minutes after three. Then he remembered Ben Collins and his sharp knife and he let the phone ring. He closed the door behind him.

Paul Smithers lived on the outskirts of Brisbane in a huge, colonial-styled house in its own grounds. The property was surrounded by a ten foot high red brick wall. As Kane drove through the electronically operated gates two large Ridgebacks came bounding through the undergrowth barking and baring their teeth. Kane drove slowly up to the front carport and waited until Paul Smithers came out and called off the dogs.

The Ridgebacks obeyed his commands instantly and lay on the concrete watching Kane, their saliva-covered tongues hanging out of their mouths, as he got out of the car.

Paul led the way into the study. He indicated a leather chair in front of the desk with a wave of his hand. 'Drink?' he asked.

'Whisky, straight, thanks Paul,' said Kane.

He watched Paul as he went over to the portable bar in front of the bookcase. He thought to himself that Paul really enjoyed the good things of life. He turned and looked at the photograph on the desk of his wife, with their high-powered launch in the background. Kane knew that Paul's wife was fifteen years younger than her husband and that he had married her on the rebound after his first wife had died almost six years before. Paul was the product of hard work. He had risen from a rank and file insurance salesman to the Company's General Manager in a comparatively short period of time.

Paul handed the glass to Kane and then walked around the desk and sat in his black leather swivel chair. 'Now, Kane,' he said, taking a sip of his drink. 'Start at the beginning.'

Kane crossed his legs. 'A contact of mine, a smalltime criminal named Danny Hurst came and saw me soon after I got back from Townsville late this afternoon saying he had some important information to sell me. I've bought stuff off him before but usually it's just run-of-the-mill. This time he hit the jackpot . . . '

'I'm sorry to interrupt but the name

sounds familiar. Let me think. Yes, there was a flash on the late television news. That was the name of a man killed in a tram accident in town tonight. Daniel Hurst, that was it!'

'I was going to get to that. It wasn't an accident, he was more or less forced off.'

'Really!' Paul Smithers' eyebrows rose about half an inch. 'Carry on.'

'Danny Hurst was working evenings at a printing works out on Bank Street. I've just been out there. The place is being run as a cover by the Big Boy and his organisation.'

Paul's eyebrows shot up again. 'The Big Boy, eh? I didn't know he was still active. Nothing's been heard of him or his organisation since, what, last January. So he's back in circulation again?'

Kane nodded his head. 'He's taken us for a ride before, but not this time. We can nip his scheme in the bud before it gets started. Danny Hurst overheard a conversation at this printing works on an extension phone. He managed to hear the whole story.'

'That was a piece of luck for us,' said Smithers.

'But not for him. Danny couldn't keep his mouth closed. He was deliberately silenced, that's for sure. Here's how this swindle's going to work. Every year Cheyney's offer one million to one odds on anyone forecasting the first three places in the Melbourne Cup. Now, these bets have to be placed weeks before the running of the race, when there's about seventy-five horses in the field. As you know, there's only twenty-four accepted for the actual race.'

'It sounds like an impossible bet, Kane.'

'Not quite. The permutation on seventy-five horses works out around the 400,000 mark. That means there's about 400,000 different forecasts, one of which will be the correct one. Now, here's what the Big Boy plans. By using funds he gets out of the gambling public from all over Australia, by offering to double their money, he'll cover those 400,000 bets. That means we'll have to cover our policy with Cheyney's. One million dollars! But he won't be paying back these punters. He'll be pocketing the lot.'

'I'm beginning to follow you, Kane. It's complicated but very clever.'

'Not only will we have to pay out a million dollars but by being associated with this policy our Company could get a bad name. If we were to cancel the policy then Cheyney's would automatically drop their offer. It's as easy as that! And the police might be able to get a lead through this printing works.'

Paul Smithers got up and began pacing around the study. He held his hands clasped behind his back. 'Yes,' he said, eventually. 'We'll have to cancel the policy. That's Number One on the list. Now what's all this about somebody gunning for you? I don't like the sound of it.'

Kane finished his drink and placed the glass on the edge of the desk. 'Danny Hurst was asking $500 for the information and I agreed. I gave him a hundred on account and arranged to meet him at a nightclub later to give him the rest. He never turned up. It wasn't like Danny so I started looking around. I went out to this printing works on Bank Street and got jumped.'

'Does that account for the sticking plaster on your neck?' asked Paul.

Kane nodded his head. 'Yes. I managed to get away from one of them but then played into the other's hands. He was waiting in the back of my car. He was very handy with a knife. I'd like to catch up with him one day. His name's Ben Collins.'

'What happened then?' asked Paul, fixing Kane another drink.

'I was being taken for what the Americans call 'the last ride'. Luckily I managed to attract the attention of a traffic cop and he saved the day by pulling us up. I got stuck a couple of times in the neck but otherwise I'm okay.'

'Do you think he would have killed you, Kane?'

'I'm sure of it. Right then I was the only one who knew of the scheme except Danny, and he was already dead. If they could have silenced me then they could have carried on.' Kane reached into his inside pocket and got out the printed pamphlets. 'Here's what I found at the printing works. They've had thousands of these things printed.'

Paul Smithers took the pamphlets and read one through. When he had finished he tapped the paper with his finger. 'It's well written, Kane. A lot of people would have fallen for it. Two to One is good odds, especially when the promoters say it's guaranteed.'

'I'll say,' Kane replied.

Paul Smithers walked around the study once more. He stopped and stood looking at an original oil painting on the far wall for a few seconds, then turned and faced Kane.

'Right. Now let me sum up. First of all, we'll cancel the policy with Cheyney's. That will put paid to that side of this business. Now we get to you. From what you've told me your life's in danger. This man, Ben Collins, will most probably have another go at you even though he'll have guessed you've already put in your report. He sounds like the type who'll bear a grudge and want to even the score. Right?'

'He was definitely a professional, Paul,' said Kane.

'Here's what I'm going to suggest you

do. Get out of Brisbane and lie low until the heat's off. We'll get the police on to this. After a couple of weeks you'll be safe to return.'

'Well,' said Kane. 'I agree that it's not too healthy around here for me at present but this is my job. I'm not in the habit of running away. That's what I'm being paid for . . .'

Paul held up his hand. 'Kane, you've done your job as far as I'm concerned. You've saved the Company a lot of money, a hell of a lot of money. That's what we expect from our investigators. But once they've done their job we don't want them hanging around particularly if there's a chance of them getting killed. No, I still think it's a good idea if you got out of Brisbane, in fact, out of the country. How about Fiji? You're about due for a spot of leave.'

'You're the boss, Paul. If you think it's a good idea then I'll go along with it.'

'Well, that's settled then. Call in at the office tomorrow morning around ten with a written report covering this whole episode. After that you're free to take off. I'll have Jansen get your tickets and traveller's cheques. See her after you've given me the report. And watch your step Kane.'

Kane shook the General Manager by the hand and then let himself out. He felt as if a load had been lifted off his shoulders. Paul would see that the policy was cancelled and place all the evidence before the police, and, besides, a paid holiday was just what he needed. As he climbed into his car he turned and looked through the lighted window at Paul Smithers in the study. He was sitting at his desk, writing busily on a sheet of paper.

As the car rolled down the driveway Kane saw the dogs bounding up towards him. They snapped at the wheels and Kane wound up the window. They stopped as he made the gates, not venturing beyond them.

Kane drove quickly along the deserted roads into Brisbane. There was a decided chill in the air. It was almost four.

At the Berkeley he told the night porter to give him a call at eight. As he opened the door to his suite he saw that there was a note stuck under the door. He held it

up to his nose and sniffed it. The
envelope was scented.

Darling,
  Have rung and rung you, but no
answer. Can't sleep and am feeling like
talking to you. Please come around directly
you get back from wherever it is you've
gone. The time doesn't matter.
                    Love,
                    Yvonne.

Kane laughed. And he thought it might
have been Ben Collins ringing up. He
took a coin and flicked it up in the air; if
heads turned up he'd go around; if tails,
he'd go to bed.
  The coin landed up tails. He began to
untie his tie, then stopped and looked at
himself in the mirror. He said aloud: 'And
why the hell not?'
  The last object he saw as he went out
were his black silk pyjamas neatly folded
on the bed.
  He sighed and walked towards the
elevator.

5

The Lull Before the Storm

Kane lay on the beach and watched as the waves broke over the reef.

The hotel he was staying at was famous for its location, situated along the coast from Suva and close to Nandi, the International Airport. The hotel and bures, Fijian styled houses, were nestled on a beach which was sheltered from the elements in a natural cove. It was a place for the weary traveller, the honeymoon couple who demanded privacy or the adventurer who was looking for fun. All could be accommodated for at the Korulevu Beach Hotel.

Kane sat up and turned his head to look along the beach. A Fijian, carrying a tray, was coming along the sand.

'Hi, there, Samisoni,' shouted Kane. 'You've found me okay?'

'Yes, Mr. Kane,' replied the Fijian,

offering the tray to him. 'I knew you'd be down by the tree someplace.'

'Thanks,' said Kane, taking the tall glass off the tray and signing the chit.

The Fijian smiled and turned to leave. Kane called him back. 'Say, Samisoni, you may be able to help me. I was by the reception desk this morning when a middle-aged couple and a young lady booked in . . . '

'You mean Mr. and Mrs. McClelland and their American friend?'

'That could be them,' replied Kane. 'What do you know about them?'

'Not much. They're staying until next Monday. Is there something I can do?'

'I was thinking it would be nice if they were seated at the table next to me at dinner. That way I might be able to get to know them.'

The Fijian laughed. He said: 'I know the head waiter in the dining-room. I'll have a word with him.'

Kane lay soaking up the sun until it began to get dark. He finished off his lazy day by having a quick swim. After a rub down, he picked up his gear and made his way to his bure.

He threw his towel and flight bag on to the divan and went over to the refrigerator. He took out a can of Foster's lager and punctured two holes in the lid. He took it with him into the bathroom.

Kane had a cold shower and then walked into the lounge with a towel tied around his waist. He looked at his wristwatch and saw that it was just after six. He thought he'd get dressed and then go down to the bar for a quick drink before dinner.

Kane had time for a couple of Martinis in the Bamboo Room before dinner was announced. He signed his bar chits and got off his stool.

'Good evening, Mr. Kane,' said the head waiter, as he came forward to meet Kane. 'I must apologise to you before I show you to your seat. Unfortunately I have sat somebody else at your table. Perhaps you wouldn't mind sitting at another one tonight.'

Kane looked at the head waiter and detected a slight wink in his left eye. Kane smiled and nodded his head.

The head waiter pulled out a chair for him and said: 'I hope this is to your liking, Mr. Kane?'

Kane looked around. The table across the narrow aisle was set for three. He looked up. 'Yes, I think this will do me fine.'

He had nearly finished the raw fish entrée when the middle-aged couple and the young woman arrived at their table.

She was more striking than he had first thought. She was tall and willowy with long, well-brushed hair which flowed over her shoulders. She was wearing a simple, black cocktail dress. There were no rings on her fingers. The man was vaguely familiar but Kane couldn't place him. Maybe, he thought, their paths had crossed at some stage in life.

Kane finished his dinner and refilled his glass from the wine bottle. He leant back in his chair and looked out of the window. The moon was just rising from behind the coconut trees and was reflecting on the water's edge, where some small waves were breaking. It was a truly beautiful night.

Then a strange thing happened. The man got up and walked over to Kane's table. He said: 'Forgive me for disturbing you, but my wife and I are sure we know you. My name is McClelland. I have a business in Sydney which, I believe I'm right in saying, you investigated after it was burnt down two years ago. Am I right?'

Kane pushed back his chair and rose. He said: 'You're dead right, Mr. McClelland. It's coming back to me now.' Kane shook him by the hand. 'The name's Kane. Adam Kane. Yes, I only met you briefly at the site. It was just a routine check. I trust things are better on our second meeting?'

'Much better, thank you. I was very pleased with the way your firm paid up so quickly. It was a sticky time. Why don't you come over and meet my wife and a friend of ours?'

'It would be a pleasure,' said Kane, picking up his cigarettes and putting them in his pocket.

Mrs. McClelland held out her hand for

Kane. She smiled at him. 'Mr. Kane, I would like you to meet a friend of ours from the United States, Miss Elaine Walters.'

Kane looked at the girl. 'I'm very pleased to meet you, Miss Walters,' he said.

Elaine smiled back at him as she shook his hand.

McClelland said: 'Perhaps you'd like to join us for coffee in the Bamboo Room?'

'I would,' Kane replied.

'Over here on business?'

'No, pleasure,' replied Kane. 'A well earnt holiday.'

'Well, you've come to the right spot.'

Kane moved Elaine's chair back for her and she slipped her arm through his as they walked towards the door. She said, softly: 'I hear there's a dance tonight?'

'That's right. In the Bamboo Room,' said Kane.

The head waiter held the door open for them and Kane patted him on the shoulder as they went out.

The three piece band was playing a

haunting Fijian War Cry softly and the room had filled up considerably since before dinner.

After they'd finished coffee and the table was cleared they ordered drinks. The band was still playing and Kane asked Elaine for a dance. She smiled and rose from the table. She took hold of Kane's hand as they walked out on to the floor. Then she nestled into his arms.

They danced together for most of the evening. Mr. and Mrs. McClelland went to bed early and waved to them as they went out of the door.

'Nice people,' said Kane. 'How did you come to know them?'

'It's a long story. During the war my father was stationed out in Port Moresby, New Guinea, as a surgeon and he met Mr. McClelland there. They wrote to each other after the war and then his daughter came over to the States for a visit. This year I'm their guest. They met me at Nandi this morning. We're flying down to Sydney next week sometime.'

'I didn't know Mr. McClelland was interested in medicine.'

'He isn't. You may have noticed he walks with a slight limp,' said Elaine.

Kane nodded his head. 'It's hardly noticeable.'

'He was shot by a Japanese sniper. Dad fixed him up at the field hospital. He always says it was one of his most satisfactory operations. Apparently the other doctors were preparing to amputate but Dad thought he could save it, and as you can see, he was right.'

'And they've been writing to each other since then?' asked Kane.

Elaine nodded her head. The band finished the tune they were playing and put down their instruments. Kane led Elaine back to the table.

Elaine said: 'Let's take our drinks out on to the veranda, Adam. It's getting too warm in here.'

They sat talking about many subjects, taking in the beauty of the tropical night, until the dance finished. Then they sat, holding hands and watching the moon shine down on the sea.

'Feeling tired?' asked Kane.

'No, just the opposite,' Elaine replied. 'I

feel wide awake. Let's go for a walk along the beach.'

They went down to the sea and walked slowly along the sand. Kane put his arms around Elaine's shoulder and she nestled in closer to him. The tide was out and parts of the reef were showing, gleaming in the moonlight, each time a wave crashed over them.

They walked past the tree where Kane had sunbathed that day and followed the curve of the beach until they came to a stone wall.

'Look's as if this is as far as we go,' said Kane, picking Elaine up by the waist and lifting her on to the wall. 'We'll sit here for a while.' He jumped up and sat beside her.

Kane looked around at the scene, taking in the gently swaying palm trees, the waves cascading down on the near-by reef, the full moon and lastly, at the beautiful girl beside him. He thought that this was what he was slaving away for in Australia; the chance to retire to such a place as this.

He turned and put his arm around her

shoulder. She closed her eyes and waited for him to kiss her. She had been waiting for the moment all evening.

Later, much later, she asked: 'Adam, how long are you staying in Fiji?'

'It all depends,' replied Kane. 'Maybe a week, maybe longer.'

'You'll be down in Sydney, sometime, won't you?' she asked.

'Too right! Will you be staying with the McClellands?'

'Yes. You know, Adam, I have a suspicion I'm really going to enjoy my stay in this part of the world.'

Kane looked at his wristwatch. The minute hand was approaching the hour. He held his wrist up to his eyes and saw that it was nearly four.

'I must get you back to your bure. The houseboy will be bringing you your cup of morning tea soon.'

They walked up through the palm trees and found the concrete pathway which led to the bures. Elaine found her key and opened the door. She turned around and kissed Kane. She said: 'Thank you for a wonderful evening. I don't think, somehow, that I'll make breakfast in the morning so I'll see you on the beach around eleven.'

'That's a date,' said Kane, releasing his hold on her. He waited until she had closed the door and then turned and made his way slowly to his own bure.

Kane looked in his pocket for his key, found it and inserted it in the lock. He turned the key but the lock didn't click open. He thought back to when he had last left the bure. He could have sworn he'd locked the door after him.

He opened the door and entered. He felt along inside the door for the lightswitch. He was just about to push it down when a heavy object hit him on the head. The blow stunned him for an instant and he crawled across the room shaking his head to clear it. He could hear a man breathing heavily by the doorway and could hear his hand sliding up and down the wall surface looking for the lightswitch.

Kane shook his head again and grabbed hold of the settee and drew himself up. He could feel blood from the cut on his head oozing down his forehead. He wiped it away with the back of his hand before it got into his eyes and blinded him. He stumbled towards the refrigerator and searched along the top for the bottle of water he knew was there. His hand enclosed around it and he changed his grip to around the neck. He held it in his hand and went searching for his assailant.

Just as he got to the door, the lights went on and Kane had a fleeting glimpse of a man with a revolver in his hand. Attached to the barrel was a silencer. Kane brought down the bottle on the man's arm and he dropped the revolver.

Kane brought up his knee into the man's stomach. The man went down on one knee and hooked his arms around Kane's legs, bringing him down with a crash.

They rolled across the floor until they reached the far corner of the room. Kane managed to get on top of his attacker and brought his right arm around in a judo chop. The man's head snapped back and hit the skirting board. He lay still.

Kane got slowly to his feet and wiped the blood out of his eyes. He went across to the door and picked up the revolver and stuck it into his trouser belt.

He went over to the telephone and picked up the receiver. He held it to his ear, then threw it back on to the cradle and followed the cord with his eyes. It had been torn out from the wall socket.

Kane went over to his attacker again and looked at him. He was about his own age. He had a thin scar above his right eye and had two teeth missing in his lower jaw. Kane rolled him over with his foot and then searched him. He took out the man's wallet and opened it up. Inside was an Australian passport. The man's name was Kordina. Kane studied the photograph and then looked at the man on the floor again. His trained eye told him at a glance that it wasn't the same person. It was a close resemblance but not the same. The passport was a clever forgery.

Kane searched around for a tie and bound the man's wrists behind his back. Then he went out of the bure and walked along the concrete pathway towards the reception desk. He thought that this was a case for the police.

He opened the swing doors and was just about to enter the large reception area. The desk was around the corner but a mirror, hung on the wall at an angle, made it possible for a person to see the desk from the door. Kane glanced into it and then stopped dead in his tracks. Leaning across the counter, talking to the young part-European desk clerk, was Ben Collins, complete with a matchstick between his teeth.

Kane felt behind him and pushed open the door quietly and let himself out. A thought flashed through his brain as he hurriedly made his way back to his bure. He wondered how they had known that he was in Fiji. Only a few people knew where he was and all of them were in the employ of the West Pacific Insurance Company.

His thoughts were interrupted as he returned to his bure. His blue tie, the one he had tied his attacker's wrists up with, was lying across the back of the settee.

Kane took the revolver out of his belt. He decided that the odds were against him. He thought it might be just a little bit safer if he left the hotel. Things were getting too hot for him at Korulevu.

6

Trapped!

Kane quickly packed his suitcase. He took a quick look around the bure and then let himself out. He made his way across some waste ground behind the hotel to the road.

He began walking in the direction of Suva. Five minutes later a truck came around the bend, its headlights piercing the early morning darkness. Kane went into the centre of the road and flagged it down.

The driver brought the truck to a standstill. Kane walked around to the driver's side and looked up into the cab at the Fijian driver.

'Bula,' said Kane. 'Say, can you give me a lift into Suva? I've got stranded out here somehow.'

'Sure, boss,' replied the Fijian. 'Jump up into the cab.'

Kane climbed up and closed the door. The Fijian engaged the gears and got the truck rolling.

'Woman trouble, mister?' asked the Fijian.

Kane looked at him. Then he smiled. 'What makes you say that?'

'Your chin's covered in lipstick. The blood on your forehead looks like you had a fight. Husband come back early?'

Kane got out his handkerchief and spat onto it. He started to wipe the congealed blood off his forehead. 'You could call it trouble, I guess,' Kane said. 'But it's not woman trouble. I only wish it was. I'd be able to look after it.'

'Where are you from?' asked the Fijian.

'Sydney. Brisbane, the east coast of Australia.'

'Where are you staying in Suva? If you're not booked into a hotel why not come and stay with me?'

'That's kind of you, but I won't trouble you. I'll find a spot someplace,' said Kane.

'It's no trouble, mister. You come and stay with me. Maybe I can get you a girl.

95

How does that sound?'

'Right now, after a particularly rough night, it sounds terrible,' said Kane.

The Fijian laughed and got out his cigarettes. He offered one to Kane. They drove in silence for a while. Kane placed his legs up on to the dashboard and closed his eyes.

He had his eyes closed for about five minutes when the Fijian woke him. He said: 'Looks as if a car's coming up on us fast. The driver's weaving all over the place.'

Kane sat up and looked into the rearview mirror. He could just make out a car careering from side to side of the road, trying to escape the dust thrown up from the truck. The driver had his hand on the horn.

'Who's in the car?' asked Kane.

'I can't see too well, too much dust, but there seems to be two men in it.'

Kane slid off the seat and sat on the floor of the cab. He took out the revolver from underneath his jacket. He said: 'Whatever you do, friend, don't stop this truck. I have a feeling those two boys are after me. If we stop they might try to knock me off. If they do you'll be a witness and these boys don't like having witnesses around.'

'I understand you, mister. You stay down on the floor. I'll handle these bastards.'

The car drew level with the truck as the Fijian pulled over to the side of the road. One of the men wound down the window and poked his head out. 'Hey, has a car passed you during the last half-hour?' he called out.

'Yeah, there was one about ten minutes ago. Some guy driving like the clappers. He nearly ran me off the road.'

The man pulled his head back into the car and wound up the window. The Fijian slowed right down to let the car get well ahead so that he didn't have to drive in the flying dust.

'Thanks,' said Kane. 'You handled that nicely.'

'Anytime, mister. I've been in a few scraps myself. Those fellows looked as if they meant business, especially the one chewing on a match. He looked a mean type to me.'

They reached the outskirts of Suva just before eight in the morning. The Fijian driver saw a car which resembled the one that had passed them earlier that morning and Kane got down on the floor again. They drove up to a village named Samabula. The driver took a turning to the left and pulled up outside a Fijian bure with a corrugated iron roof.

'Mister,' he said. 'You get out here and take your suitcase into that bure. A hotel wouldn't be safe for you at present. I'll have to go down and leave this truck at the works and then I'll be back. Tell my girl-friend you're a friend of mine. My name's Atunaisa. And behave yourself, eh?'

Kane waved his hand and walked up to the bure. He knocked on the door, then opened it and walked in.

A door opened and a young girl came out. She was wearing a red-coloured sulu tied around her waist. She had nothing else on. Her eyes opened wide when she saw Kane.

Kane said quickly: 'It's all right. Atunaisa told me to come in.'

When Kane had finished explaining a large smile spread across her face. She bent down and picked up his suitcase and took it into a room. She beckoned for him to follow.

The room was very small but it had a bed and a couple of sheets. Kane turned to the Fijian girl and smiled his thanks. She closed the door and left him.

Atunaisa returned to the bure as Kane finished shaving and they all sat down for breakfast. Atunaisa asked him to sit at the head of the table.

'Sainimari doesn't speak much English,' Atunaisa said, indicating the girl. 'But if you speak slowly she should be able to make out what you want.'

'I'll remember that,' said Kane. 'She's a nice looking lass.'

'Yeah, I've asked her if she knows of a friend who can move in here for a few days.'

Kane put up his hands. He said: 'Look, Atunaisa. I'm very grateful for being put up like this. You've saved me a lot of worry. If I registered into a hotel these men would soon find me. I appreciate your gesture but I haven't got time to hang around. I've got to get back to Australia as quickly as I can.'

'Suit yourself,' replied Atunaisa. 'I just thought that a young man like you wouldn't want to be alone at nights.'

Atunaisa went to his room after breakfast and the girl went with him. Kane could hear them laughing together. He lit a cigarette.

After ten minutes he yawned and ran his hand over his forehead. All of a sudden he felt the strain of the night before. He decided that a spot of bed would do him some good.

He lay on the bed, turned over on to his stomach and let his arms hang over both sides of the mattress. He was asleep within five minutes.

Atunaisa woke Kane by knocking softly on his door. 'Had a good sleep?' he asked.

'Fine,' replied Kane, rubbing his eyes.

'Not that I want to interfere with your business,' said the Fijian. 'But what do you plan doing?'

'I have to get back to Australia. What's the time now?' asked Kane.

'Nearly half past four in the afternoon,' said Atunaisa, picking up Kane's watch off the floor. 'How are you going to get out of Fiji?'

'Fly out,' said Kane. 'Where's the nearest phone booth from here?'

'There's one at Fong Hoon's, down at the main road,' said the Fijian. 'If you hurry you should be able to get there before they close.'

Kane walked briskly down the dusty road until he came to the main road. He thought that the chances of being spotted by the two men in Samabula were very slight. He decided that he would be safe on the outskirts of Suva but would have to use caution if he ever went into town.

He found the store and pushed open the door. Kane picked up the small telephone book and started leafing through the pages looking for a Travel Agent. He found that there was one listed under Burns Philp. He dialled the number.

A man's voice answered the phone. Kane said: 'I have to get out of Fiji urgently. It's very important. When is the next plane flying out of Nandi for Sydney?'

'There's one tomorrow morning at 5.15 a.m. I could get you on that one. A connecting flight leaves Nausori this evening.'

'That sounds like the one I want,' said Kane. 'Look, is it possible for me to come and see you right away?'

'Surely, come right down. We're right in the centre of town.'

Kane replaced the receiver and went back to the counter. He bought some cigarettes and cashed a traveller's cheque. He selected a picture postcard from the rack and scribbled a hurried note to Elaine, explaining his sudden departure from the hotel. He promised that he would look her up in Sydney.

He made his way back to Atunaisa's house. He found them both sitting outside in the cool of the early evening. 'Come inside for a second, Atu,' said Kane.

Atunaisa got up from the orange box and followed Kane inside the bure.

'Listen, Atunaisa,' Kane began. 'I might

have to leave here in a hurry. Right now I have to go into Suva to see about my ticket. First of all I want you to accept this money,' he put his hand in his pocket and took out a ten dollar note, 'for all you've done for me.'

Atunaisa interrupted him. He said: 'I don't want any money for what I've done. It is a Fijian custom to help visitors to our islands.'

'Well, that's a real nice custom,' said Kane. 'Will you accept it if I give it to you as a gift? I'll tell you what; take Sainimari out and buy her a dress or something. Buy something you've always wanted for your bure. How about that?'

'Well,' said Atunaisa slowly. 'I don't know . . . '

Kane stuffed the note in Atunaisa's top shirt pocket and slapped him on the back. He said: 'I wish I didn't have to leave these islands so quickly. I'd like to have a few drinks with you.'

'You can always come back,' said the Fijian. 'My front door will always be open.'

'I'll remember that,' said Kane. He

went into his room and took down his lightweight tropical jacket from off the nail behind the door. He put it on and then undid his suitcase. Kane took out the revolver and unscrewed the silencer, throwing it back into the suitcase. He opened up the gun and checked the chambers. He saw that two cartridges had already been fired. A slight shiver went down his spine as he realised how close he had been to death at the hotel.

He stuck the revolver in the waistband of his trousers and buttoned up his coat. He took out his passport and private papers and stuck them all in his back pocket. He left his suitcase on the bed to be picked up later and then went outside.

An empty taxi overtook him on the road and he flagged it down. The driver dropped Kane outside Stinson's at the traffic lights. The Travel Agents were on the opposite side of the road.

Kane crossed and looked in the window of the office. A light was burning over one of the desks and a bald-headed man was studying some papers. Kane knocked on the door.

The man got up and opened the door. Kane shook his hand and apologised for keeping him past his usual working hours.

'Think nothing of it, old boy,' said the Agent. 'Now, what was it you wanted?'

Kane told him he had to get out of Fiji urgently. The Agent opened a drawer of his desk and took out some forms and ticket butts.

Kane relaxed in the leather chair and brought out his cigarettes. He thought that with a little luck he might make it.

The Agent asked for Kane's passport and Kane was about to take it out of his pocket when the telephone rang.

'Funny,' said the Travel Agent. 'It's for you.'

Kane froze. He automatically took the receiver from the outstretched hand. He placed it to his ear. A voice said: 'Well, well, well, Mister bloody Kane, we've got you this time. That's the first place we started watching. Directly you leave that office you'll be followed and then, when it gets dark . . . ' Ben Collins let a weird chuckle escape from his throat.

Kane slammed the receiver down. He

got up and looked out of the window at the street outside. Leaning against the wall opposite was Kordina, the man who had attacked him at the hotel.

'Is there a back way out of this place?' Kane asked the startled Travel Agent.

'Yes. Why?'

'Good. I'm sorry to have troubled you. I won't be needing that ticket any longer. I'm going to have to change my plans.'

'Are you in some kind of trouble?'

'You're not kidding!' replied Kane, taking out the revolver and making his way to the back of the office.

7

Money Well Spent

Kane opened the back door slowly. He looked up and down the narrow, dustbin-littered alleyway. He was looking for Ben Collins. Somehow he imagined that he would be checking the alleyway.

There was no sign of him. Kane held the revolver at the ready and walked quickly towards the exit. He could see that it came out at a small creek. It was getting dark.

Kane wondered what he should do. From what Ben hinted, it seemed as if there could be more than just two of the organisation watching and waiting for him. If, Kane thought, they were watching the Travel Agents then they would also be watching the docks to see whether he jumped a ship.

Kane stood on the corner of the street. He cursed himself for the way he was acting. He thought that to run away from danger was not like him. Usually he faced up to it, hit it on the head.

A Fijian girl came up to the corner of the street. She stared at Kane and walked slowly past him. She smiled up at him. She said: 'Hallo. Are you lost?'

'Er, what did you say?' asked Kane.

'You looking for some place to go?'

Kane thought quickly. Here was a way to get off the streets in a hurry. 'Yes, you know of a place?'

The girl said: 'I'm just off to a party. You like to come?'

'Sure,' answered Kane, quickly.

The girl took his hand and they walked along the street. She said: 'It's a long way out. Shall we take a taxi?'

'Okay,' smiled Kane, looking up and down the street.

The girl smiled. She said: 'How about a case of beer? We could get it on the way.'

'Right. Let's hurry,' said Kane. The fourth car to pass them was an empty taxi and the Fijian girl signalled it to stop. They both climbed into the back seat.

They stopped at a liquor store to buy a

case of beer and then continued out along the Lami road. They pulled up, after ten minutes of fast driving, at a dilapidated house with a rusty corrugated iron roof.

'Here we are,' said the Fijian girl. 'Will you pay the driver?'

Kane took out a note and handed it to the Indian taxi driver. He took the case of beer out and put it under his arm.

The door to the house was wide open and the sounds of a guitar came to them. The girl waited for him at the doorway and then put her arm through his.

'What's your name?' she asked.

'Adam. Adam Kane. What's yours?'

'Just call me Queenie,' said the girl. 'Everyone knows me as Queenie.'

'Everyone?' asked Kane, raising his eyebrows.

They walked in and entered a large living-room. Sitting on the floor were a crowd of Fijian men and women. Two men were sitting on a window ledge, one was playing the guitar. They all looked up as Queenie and Kane entered.

Queenie waved her hand and said: 'Bula, everyone. This is my carshine for the night, Adam Kane.'

Some of the men waved to Kane and one of them indicated a spot on the floor where he could sit down. Kane climbed over the outstretched legs to the space beside a thick-set Fijian. The Fijian had a slim moustache on his upper lip and was wearing dark glasses. Kane thought that he had made a bad choice in coming out to the house. These boys looked tough!

Kane sat down and a newly opened can of beer was placed in his hands. The Fijian next to him asked: 'Where are you from, mister?'

Kane told him.

'How did you get to meet Queenie?' asked another Fijian.

'It wasn't hard,' replied Kane. 'We met on a corner of a street.'

The Fijian let out a laugh. He said: 'That's Queenie. She's the busiest hustler in Suva.'

Kane relaxed a bit. He looked to see where Queenie was and saw that she was talking to a huge Fijian in the far corner of the room. The Fijian had his arm over her shoulder. Kane thought that she was a load off his mind.

Another girl, a pretty, pert part-Island girl with long flowing hair was watching Kane. She got up and walked across the room and sat down next to him. She said: 'Hallo, Adam. It looks as if you've lost your girl-friend. My name's Maria. Can I have one of your cigarettes?'

Kane took out his packet and gave her one. He lit it for her. Kane watched her and then looked around the room again. He noticed that Queenie was leaving the room with the huge Fijian. He felt somewhat relieved.

'You came with Queenie, didn't you, Adam?' the girl asked.

'That's right. I met her downtown. I had to get out of Suva in a hurry.'

'Why was that? Have you done something wrong?'

'No, nothing wrong.' He wondered how he could tell the girl. He thought up a story and decided to try it out on her. He said: 'There's two men, both private detectives, who are looking for me. They want to question me about a robbery in Australia. Somehow I have the idea that if they catch up with me they'll frame me.'

'And these men are here in Fiji?'

'Right,' said Kane. 'They're watching the airport at Nandi and the docks here. I've no way of getting out. But I have to get back to Sydney as quickly as possible. It's the only way I can prove my innocence.'

'But how do you plan getting out if they're watching like that?' asked Maria, slipping her arm through his.

'If I knew I wouldn't be sitting here, I'd be on my way,' said Kane. 'I had hoped I might meet somebody here who could help me. Queenie told me a few of the men worked on the wharf and might know of a ship I could get on.'

'That's right. Johnnie and Jake work there. They might know how to get you on to a boat.'

Maria looked around and then spotted one of the men. She called out his name and spoke to him in Fijian. The man got up slowly from the floor and walked over to them.

'This is Jake,' said Maria. 'He might be able to help you, Adam.'

Kane opened up his cigarettes and handed them around. He studied the Fijian's face as he lit his cigarette. He told him the same story as he had told Maria. He concluded: ' . . . and if you could help me get out, and by that I mean in the next day or two, I'd make it well worth your while.'

'How much?' asked Jake.

'Say twenty dollars,' replied Kane.

Jake stubbed out his cigarette. Then he lifted his head and looked at Kane. He said: 'If you had come a couple of days earlier I could have helped you.'

'How do you mean?' asked Kane.

'There was a yacht here due to sail for Auckland, New Zealand. They were looking for crew members and also a couple of paying passengers. The captain asked us if we knew of anyone.'

'The yacht left the other day?' asked Maria.

'Yep, they said they were going down to the mouth of the Rewa for a while.'

'Where's that?' asked Kane.

'Ah, it's a place about thirty miles out of Suva,' said the Fijian. 'There's a couple of villages there and a beach.'

Kane felt a tingle of excitement go through his veins. It looked as if there was a way out; a way out which would take time, but at least a way which Ben Collins and Kordina wouldn't know about. 'How do you get to this place?' asked Kane.

'You'd have to go by boat,' said Maria.

'Yep, you'd have to go to Wainibokasi at the head of the river and hire a boat from there,' said Jake.

'Do you think I'd be able to get one at this time of night?' asked Kane.

'Man, you really are in a hurry,' said Jake.

'I'll come with you, if you like,' said Maria. 'I've been down there before and know some of the villagers.'

'That would be great if you could,' said Kane. 'Tell me, is there a phone here? I'll get a taxi.'

Kane used the phone and then gave Jake the twenty dollars he had promised him. Minutes later a taxi drew up outside the house and Maria and Kane walked down the pathway towards it.

Kane opened the door for Maria and then climbed in beside her. He told the driver to go to Wainibokasi.

The driver took the road out to Nausori. Maria nestled into Kane's shoulder and went to sleep. Kane looked down at her and stroked her hair. He thought that his memory of Fiji would definitely be one of the helpfulness of the Islanders towards him. Everyone he had met had put themselves out to help him, without enquiring too deeply into his troubles.

The only people awake at Wainibokasi were two taxi drivers who were playing cards on the bus seat. Maria went over and talked to them. One of them pointed to the centre one of the three stores there.

Kane knocked hard on the wooden door of the store. He listened with his ear against the wood and heard a mumbled oath come from inside.

An Indian, his eyes half closed with sleep, poked his head out. He looked at Kane.

'You speak to him, Maria. Tell him that I have to get down to one of the villages at the mouth of the river tonight. Tell him it's urgent and I'll pay twice the usual charge.'

Maria spoke quickly to the Indian. When she mentioned about paying twice the usual charge, the Indian stood erect. He said something to Maria and then closed the door.

'What did he say?' asked Kane.

'He told us to wait while he got dressed.'

Five minutes later the Indian came out of his store carrying the red fuel tank for an outboard. They watched him as he climbed down the steep steps to the landing stage and into one of the moored boats.

Kane helped Maria in and sat next to her near the bows. The Indian untied the rope, got out a long pole and punted out into mid-stream. He connected the hose to the engine, squeezed the bulb pump and then pulled the cord. The outboard spluttered into life. Kane looked at his wristwatch and saw that it was close to two.

The Indian opened the throttle and the

boat jumped forward and the bows lifted out of the water. Soon they were planing.

After three-quarters of an hour they turned a bend and ahead of them the flashing light of a lighthouse beamed out. 'We're nearly there,' said Maria, as she saw the light.

The Indian turned the handle throttle of the outboard and cut down the speed. Moored ahead of them, with its stern light showing, was a yacht.

'There she is, Adam,' shouted Maria, pointing at the yacht. 'You've made it! It hasn't sailed yet!'

Kane felt a surge of excitement go through his body. Somewhere deep down in his body he was beginning to enjoy the thrill of the chase. It was exhilarating to outwit and outrun a large organisation; to match his skill against theirs.

The Indian cut the engine and they drifted on to the sandy beach. Kane jumped over the side and pulled the boat the last few yards. A dog started barking in the near-by village.

'I know some of the villagers here,' said Maria. 'We could send the boatman back.

I'll make my way up river tomorrow. There's always a boat going up and down.'

'Okay,' said Kane. He walked back to the boat and paid the Indian and told him he could return. The Indian started poling the boat out into the channel.

Kane looked at his watch. It was almost three. 'My first concern,' Kane said to Maria, 'is to make sure I can get a berth on that yacht. I see there's a small dinghy moored up the beach. I'll take it and have a word with the fellow on watch. You can see the glow of his cigarette there, at the wheel.'

'I'll give you a hand with the dinghy,' said Maria. 'Then I'll go up to the village and see if we can get a place to stay for the rest of the night.'

Kane untied the dinghy and threw the anchor into the bows. 'I'll meet you back here in about fifteen minutes. Okay?'

'Okay, Adam. Good luck!' She helped him push the dinghy down to the water's edge and then watched as he pulled on the oars towards the yacht. She wished silently that he could stay longer in Fiji.

She was just getting to know him.

She turned, when she saw him reach the yacht, and went to find her friends in the village.

8

Nowhere is Safe

Kane heard the chicken pecking away just above his ear and he opened his eyes and turned over on to his stomach. The chicken stared at him for several seconds, then scratched at a fold in the mat and continued.

Kane took his hand out from underneath the sheet and looked at his watch. It was just after six in the morning.

He got up and dressed and made his way out of the bure. He walked down to the river's edge and took off his shirt. He squatted down and cupped his hands into the salty water and washed his face.

Maria came out of one of the bures and looked around. She spotted Kane and walked down to join him. She was wearing a borrowed blue and yellow sulu wrapped around her body. Her hair was hanging loose over her brown shoulders.

'Do you have to leave, Adam?' she asked.

'I'm afraid so. We're sailing at about nine when the tide changes. I've got to go aboard and see the captain soon.'

Maria looked out at the white yacht. She had a sad look on her face . . .

Kane thought back to his visit to the yacht after the Indian had dropped them at the landing the night before. The young man who had been on watch had stood at the top of the rope ladder with his hands on his hips.

'What can I do for you, mister?' he had asked.

'When do you sail?' asked Kane.

'Tomorrow morning, early. Why?'

'Good. I want to get a passage on her. I heard in Suva that you were leaving for New Zealand.'

'The captain handles the fare side of this trip,' the young man had said. 'And I can't wake him at the moment, even if it was urgent. He got bottled tonight.'

'What do you reckon, then? Meet you back here at about seven-thirty?' Kane had asked.

'Yeah, he should be about by then. He has a marvellous way of recovering. Wish I had his stamina.'

Maria had been waiting for him and had shown him to the bure where he could sleep. They had both been tired and had turned in at once . . .

Kane looked sideways at Maria. He thought she was really beautiful in a way that was peculiar to the islands. Maria turned and faced him and took hold of his hand. She said: 'Promise me, Adam, you'll come back soon. I want to see you again.'

'I'll try,' Kane replied. 'I'll try hard. Come on, let's go for a walk.'

Maria squeezed his hand and smiled. She led him down a path to the beach. Through the pandanas trees they could see the golden sands glistening in the morning sunshine.

Kane put his arms around her shoulder and they walked in silence. He was thinking of something appropriate to say. He wanted to thank her for her help, for coming down all that way just to see that he caught the yacht. He was searching for a way in which to express his thanks. Maria brought his thoughts to a swift conclusion.

She stopped in her tracks and grabbed him around the neck and kissed him. She kissed him passionately, thrusting her body at him, nearly knocking him off balance. He didn't try to move away.

'Maria, I want to thank you for all you've . . . '

Maria put her finger to his lips. 'Don't, please, Adam. Don't spoil this moment. Kiss me again.'

Kane faltered for a brief second and then threw discretion to the wind. He knew that to thank the Island people for helping was a waste of time, they did it because it was their nature. He took Maria in his arms again.

★   ★   ★

The captain of the yacht came out of the wheelhouse as Kane clambered over the side. He was a huge man, standing about six feet tall. His face was covered with a magnificent red beard and the exposed parts of his face and arms were tanned a deep golden brown.

'You must the the chappie Flynn told me about this morning? You want to come with us to New Zealand?' he bellowed.

'Correct, captain,' replied Kane.

'As a member of the crew or as a paying passenger?'

'I've got money. I'll pay. How much is it?'

The captain scratched his chin through his beard. 'Forty dollars. How does that sound to you?'

'Suits me,' said Kane. 'I'll have to give you traveller's cheques, though. I didn't have time to cash any . . . '

'I know. Flynn told me you hadn't got any baggage. One thing about this yacht, we don't ask questions and we don't expect none. The name's Stevens, Captain Stevens to you. We've got a motley lot on board but I think you'll be able to look after yourself. You can do who and what you like as long as you don't get in the crew's way when they're working the sails. You hear?'

Kane grinned.

'Right, now you'd better get down below and get something to eat. Arthur will fix you up.'

Kate turned and looked back to the shore. Maria was still standing on the beach. Kane waved to her and she waved back. He could see that she was wiping her eyes.

He turned quickly and went down the steps into the main cabin. Seated around a large table were four men and two women. They watched him closely as he came down the stairs.

'Morning,' said Kane, looking around the table. 'I've just joined the trip. Travelling to New Zealand. The name's Kane. Adam Kane.'

★　★　★

After breakfast Kane went up on deck and sat on the stern rail. He lit a cigarette and watched as the yacht made its way through the gap in the reef.

The passengers came up from below decks and stopped and spoke to him. The last one to appear was June Belamy, the woman he had sat next to at the table.

'Hi,' she said, waving her towel at him. 'You all by your lonesome?'

'No, just thinking,' replied Kane.

'You look tired. Did that pretty girl keep you awake all last night?' she asked, giving him a wink. She went for'ards.

Kane watched her movements and wondered whether the swaying of her hips was for his benefit. He let out a sigh. He thought that the next few days were going to be heavy going. He flicked his cigarette over the rail and went down below.

Kane found his cabin and sat on the bunk. He kicked off his shoes and lay back on the sheets. He closed his eyes.

He awoke with a start and looked at his watch. It was almost twelve. Getting up from the bunk he searched his pockets for a cigarette. He lit one and then took out his wallet from his back pocket and the revolver from inside his trouser band and laid them both on the bunk.

He stood up in the cramped quarters and looked at himself in a small mirror.

His chin was covered with a gingery growth. He decided it was time he had a shower and a shave. He stripped off his clothes, tied the rough bath towel around his waist and slid open the door. He went looking to see who he could borrow a razor from.

That evening, after dinner, Flynn brought out his guitar and sat in the wardroom strumming and singing softly. The passengers sat around listening.

Kane stayed for half an hour and then excused himself and went up on deck. The evening was perfect. The heat of the day had gone and a fresh breeze was blowing. The moon was rising slowly and the few clouds reflected its brilliance on to the water. Kane went for'ard to the bows and hung on to the railing. He lit a cigarette.

He had half smoked it when he heard a movement behind him. He turned quickly and saw that it was June. She was wearing a green and white cocktail dress.

'Hi,' she yelled above the wind. 'What are you doing all by yourself.'

'I was thinking,' replied Kane. 'Just private thoughts.'

'I bet,' June replied. 'You men are all

the same. I bet you were thinking up some scheme.'

'You've got me wrong, Miss Belamy,' Kane said.

'Just look at that moon, isn't it romantic?' she said, changing the subject.

Kane winced. There was something crude about her approach. He liked to do the chasing and he found it left a nasty taste in his mouth when the roles were reversed.

'I don't think so,' he said. 'In fact, I'm finding it rather rough.'

'But there's hardly any swell.'

'Enough for me. I guess I'm just a landlubber at heart.'

'What do you mean, Adam?'

'I mean I'm going to be sea sick,' lied Kane, moving away from the bows back towards the safety of the cabins.

'Oh, dear,' said June, watching him. 'How unfortunate.'

★   ★   ★

The next day was a repetition of the first. The sun was fierce and Kane chose a spot out in the centre of the deck where he was protected from the direct sunlight by the shadow of the main sail.

Lying in front of him, on her bath towel, was June. She was pretending to read a novel but Kane could see by the way she was turning the pages that she wasn't. Kane smiled to himself. He thought it was amazing to what ends some women would go to get attention.

The peaceful noise aboard the yacht; the lapping of the waves against the hull, the creaking of the sails under strain, was broken by an alien noise. At first it sounded like a dull throbbing but soon it increased to a harsh whine. Kane put down his book and looked about the sky. He glanced back at the captain and saw that he had a pair of binoculars to his eyes.

'What's that noise, Adam?' asked June.

'Could be a plane,' replied Kane.

'It is,' said June, suddenly pointing out over the rail. 'There it is!'

Kane followed her directions and caught sight of it. It was a single engined Cessna, flying towards them at about two hundred feet.

The Cessna flew right over the yacht

and then went into a banking climb. At the top of the climb it turned around in a slow curve and came at them again.

'Is he trying to signal us?' asked June. 'He's coming very close. Do you think he's in any kind of trouble?'

'The engine sounds in good trim,' Kane replied. 'Most probably some tourist out for a trip to see some of the outlying Islands. Don't forget, we're only two days out from Fiji. That would only be about three hours away in that thing.'

The Cessna flew over the yacht again and they could feel the boat sway as the sails caught the slipstream.

'Could I have a look through your binoculars, captain?' Kane asked.

'Sure, here you are,' he replied, taking off the strap from around his neck. 'Some crazy pilot having a ball, that's all.'

Kane took the glasses and put them to his eyes. He adjusted the lenses and then swept the area.

He caught the Cessna as it was coming out of a turn. The powerful binoculars gave him a pin sharp view of the plane. He tried to focus on the pilot but the angle was such that his face was hidden by a strut. He could see, though, that there were two passengers leaning out of the near side window. One of them had a pair of binoculars to his eyes and was scanning the yacht.

Kane focused on the man and his heart skipped a beat, for there, as large as life, was Ben Collins staring right back at him. The man looking over his shoulder was the same man who had been waiting in his bure at Korulevu, Kordina.

Kane walked slowly back to his deck chair. Somehow, he thought, Ben had found out about the yacht leaving Fiji and had hired a plane just to come out to check to see if he was on it. A long shot; indeed a very long shot, and sure enough, he, Kane, hadn't been quick enough off the mark to grasp the situation. Ben had spotted him. All this scheming and quick flight were now to no avail. He could be sure of a good reception when they arrived in New Zealand.

'You don't look too well, Adam,' said June, as he picked up his book. 'Are you feeling sea sick again?'

9

Missing Piece of a Jigsaw

Kane sat on the edge of his bunk cleaning the revolver. He placed the four bullets into the chamber and then snapped the barrel shut. He placed the gun under his pillow.

He lay back on the bunk and stared at the wooden planks above him. A conversation with the captain the evening before had told him that they would make Auckland during the next two or three days, depending on the strength of the wind.

Presumably, Kane told himself, Ben Collins would be waiting for him. He decided that it would be crazy to arrive at Auckland but he wondered how the hell he could avoid it, short of commandeering the yacht.

He got up from the bunk and went up on to deck. He nodded at the captain and started walking around. He stopped half way to the bows and looked about. He had to think of something, something that was feasible once they got near port. He looked back at the captain standing at the wheel and saw, for the first time, the true position of the small dinghy.

He took his foot off the railing and walked to the stern. He lit a cigarette and then studied the dinghy. It was secured by a single rope. The davit, on which the dinghy could be swung out and lowered on, was also lashed by a single rope. Kane knelt down and studied the lashings.

He stood up and lifted a corner of the tarpaulin, which was stretched across the dinghy. Inside he could see the two oars and rowlocks. There was also a tin, containing food and emergency water, tucked under the gunwale.

Kane walked back to the bows of the yacht and selected a deck chair and sat down. He lit another cigarette and tried to work out a plan.

If, he told himself, he could lower the dinghy into the water just before they were due into Auckland, and somehow managed to row her around to land at a beach, he could avoid the reception he was sure would be waiting for him.

The whole job of lowering the dinghy, he thought, needed two persons. One could do it but only just. He wondered who he could confide in. The answer, he saw immediately, was June Belamy, the buxom American woman who had been trying her hardest to seduce him since he had joined the boat.

★   ★   ★

Arthur, the cook, put on a magnificent meal that night. He had been trailing a line over the side most of the day and just before dinner had got his first bite.

Kane put down his knife and fork and pushed his plate away. He excused himself and went along to his cabin. He sat on his bunk and smoked a cigarette. He told himself that the sooner he acted, the better.

June was standing at the bows looking out over the rail when Kane found her. She was smoking a cigarette. Kane stopped beside her and lit one himself. He put his foot on the lower rail and looked up at the sky.

Kane swallowed, then said: 'Look, June. I'm in serious trouble and I need your help. I've got to confide in somebody and you're about the only person beside the captain who'll talk to me.'

'Whatever do you mean, Adam?' asked June, seriously. 'What's going on?'

Kane took the plunge. He told her about his flight from Fiji and how he'd managed to get on the yacht. Then he told her about the plane and recognising both of the men in it. ' . . . and they'll be waiting for me once we deck,' he concluded.

'But you can't land at Auckland. Your life's in danger.'

'That's right!'

'Then what can we do?' she asked, tightening her grip on his hand.

'Well, I do have an idea,' said Kane. 'It would mean stealing the dinghy off this yacht.'

'Tell me about it, Adam.'

Kane swallowed. At the back of his

mind he wondered whether he was making the right decision. 'Suppose the night before we were to enter harbour we managed to lower the dinghy. I could most probably row to the nearest point of land . . . '

'You mean row into the shore? Oh, Adam, you'd never make it.'

'I stand an even chance, which is better odds . . . '

'Sure,' said June. 'And suppose you don't? You'd spend your last hours drifting around without a hope, for nobody would be searching for you.'

'To put your mind at rest I could contact you directly I land. How about that?'

June stared out to sea.

'Better still,' said Kane. 'If you haven't heard from me within, say, three days, then you could notify the authorities. There's enough food and water in the dinghy to last that long.'

'That would be better,' said June. 'I'll tell you what. I'm planning on spending a few days at a place called Rotorua, there's some thermal springs and stuff there. I'm booked in at a place called Moore's. You could contact me there.'

'Moore's? Right!' said Kane.

June shivered and pulled her sweater around her shoulders. She said. 'It's getting cold, Adam. Let's go down to my cabin for a drink.'

Kane held her arm and led her back to the steps leading down to the cabins. As they passed Flynn at the wheel he gave Kane a wink.

★   ★   ★

But that next night, just five hours sailing away from Auckland, Kane's plan got a nasty shock. The excitement began just after dinner.

Kane had his eyes closed and was nearly asleep in the wardroom when June came down the companionway. 'Hi,' she yelled out. 'You're missing all the fun.'

'What's up?' asked Kane, sitting up.

'There's a launch of some kind on a bearing which will make it pass close to us,' she replied. 'The captain's swearing his head off. Come up and have a look for yourself.'

Kane followed June up on deck and joined the rest of the passengers and crew at the starboard rail. June pointed to sea where the bows of a high-speed launch could be seen ploughing through the water towards them.

'It looks as if it could be a Custom's launch,' said the captain. 'I didn't realise we were so close to land. My navigation tells me I'm further out.'

Kane watched as the bows of the approaching launch cut through the waves. A powerful searchlight was switched on when it was about three hundred yards away. The beam enveloped the yacht and then swung to the bows and focused on the nameplate. The launch then turned its bows slightly so that it would cut the yacht off.

The captain yelled out orders to the crew and they ran down the deck and started hauling in the sails.

When the launch was about fifty yards away it suddenly cut its engines and swung around so that it was facing the yacht broadside on.

Kane put his foot on the rail and studied the launch. It resembled in outline one of the World War II torpedo boats with a certain amount of re-fitting on the afterdeck. The searchlight was swinging slowly along the length of the yacht. Kane strained forward and tried to read the nameplate of the launch, which was just visible in the reflection from the searchlight. He could just make out the first three letters.

'KAT . . . KATH . . . KATHLEEN,' Kane said to himself. 'That's the name of Paul Smithers' launch. What the hell's he doing out here?'

And then it all fell into place. Everything suddenly fitted into position. The parts of the deadly jigsaw which hadn't fitted up until then were now so obvious that it was a wonder he hadn't seen them before.

'Paul Smithers is the Big Boy!' said Kane out aloud. 'Why the hell didn't I think of it before? No wonder Ben Collins was on to me so quickly, Paul Smithers was one of the few people who knew I was up in Fiji!'

The searchlight struck him in the face and he turned away from the blinding glare. He stumbled down the companionway to his cabin. He threw aside the pillow and picked up the revolver. He stuck it in his trouser band and then dashed up the steps on to the deck again.

The captain was shouting at his opposite number on the launch. Kane ducked down and looked around for June. She was standing by the rail watching the launch as it drifted nearer. Kane crept around the wheelhouse and tapped her on the leg.

June turned around and peered into the darkness. Then she saw him. She hurried over and bent down. 'What's the trouble, Adam?' she asked.

'We've got to work fast,' said Kane. 'That launch and the men on board are the ones I was telling you about last night.'

'Don't be mad, Adam,' said June. 'That's a Custom's launch. The captain's just been speaking to them. They're coming aboard to search us before we go into Auckland.'

'June,' said Kane, seriously. 'That isn't a Custom's launch. That boat belongs to the head of the biggest criminal organisation in Australia. If I don't get away from here in the next few minutes, I'm as good as dead. Now, do you remember what we discussed last night?'

June went visibly paler, but she nodded her head. 'Yes, Adam, but I'm scared.'

'Well, snap out of it quickly. Come on, give me a hand.'

Kane got up and made his way towards the dinghy. Luck was with him and the crew were looking out over the railings. Kane quickly untied the rope securing the dinghy and then the davit. June helped him swing it out over the stern.

She said, hurriedly: 'Adam, you can't go out there in this small boat. You'll be drowned!'

'It's my only chance,' Kane whispered.

June started to let the rope out and the dinghy gradually went down into the sea. Kane held on to the side of the yacht and pulled himself around to the port side, out of the glare of the searchlight. He fumbled around for the rowlocks and set them into the slots, then he gently rowed around to the bows.

The launch had pulled up to within ten yards of the yacht and the crew were preparing to throw ropes across before boarding.

Kane pushed off and pulled on the oars. Just as he left the safety of the yacht's side, the searchlight swung out and caught him in the glare. Immediately there was shouting and cursing from the launch and he heard an order barked out for the engines to be started.

He pulled in the oars and took out his revolver. He judged himself to be about twenty yards away from the launch. He clicked off the safety catch and aimed at the centre of the searchlight. He held the gun steady and waited until there was a lull in the movement of the dinghy. A chance presented itself but he fired too late and the bullet thudded into the woodwork of the launch.

At the sound of his shot he heard another order being given and saw the outline of a man running along the side of the launch. The man was carrying a long slender object in his hands. He pointed it at Kane and then a burst of automatic gunfire filled the air.

Kane ducked as he saw the bullets splashing into the water beside him and only raised his head when the burst finished. He raised the revolver again and aimed at the centre of the light. He waited for the dingy to rise over the crest of a wave, then he fired.

The bullet smacked into the searchlight and the light died a slow death. The automatic opened up again but the shots were yards out.

The launch engines started with a roar and Kane could see the bows lift out of the water. The launch turned after passing the yacht and swept past him, so close that the dinghy was out of sight from the men leaning over the railings looking for him.

He let out his breath and tucked the revolver back into his trouser band. He took up the oars and bent his back getting the hell out of the way.

For the next three-quarters of an hour the launch searched the area, sometimes coming within a hundred yards of the dinghy. But the torches the men on board were using were not strong enough to penetrate the darkness.

Kane searched for the yacht. He stopped rowing and scanned the darkness but there was no sign of any lights.

He sat in the dinghy, holding the oars in his hands and looked around for about ten minutes. Then he spat over the side and started rowing smoothly in the general direction indicated by the stars.

He began thinking about the events which had happened to him since he had started on the investigation into the Melbourne Cup swindle. He thought he might as well occupy his mind with something during the remaining five hours to sunrise.

10

Illegal Entry

A Japanese fishing boat picked Kane up early the next morning. They found the dinghy floating in a current which would have taken it out into the wastes of the Pacific. Kane was wet through, hungry and visibly sea sick. He collapsed on the deck after being lifted over the railings.

The captain, a short, stocky man with thick steel-rimmed glasses perched on his nose, came down from the bridge. He took one look at Kane and then gave orders for his removal to the sick bay.

Kane slept the clock around and woke up the following morning with a splitting headache. Just after he had awakened, a Japanese officer, dressed in a white shirt and shorts, came into the cabin. The man bowed and gave Kane a tray of food.

Kane looked at the plates. On one was some raw fish, on another, a combination of green shoots. There was also a small cup of tea and this was what Kane picked up first. He smelt it and then took a sip. It was lukewarm, but sweet. He drank it down slowly.

The officer returned later with Kane's clothing neatly folded over his arm. They had been washed and ironed. The officer placed them over the back of a chair and then looked at Kane. He said: 'You put on clothes, then follow me. Captain wants to speak to you. Okay?'

The captain of the Japanese fishing boat rose as Kane was shown into a cabin beside the bridge and bowed in the traditional manner. Kane bowed back.

'A very strange case,' said the captain, in a decided American drawl. 'What, may I ask, were you doing out in these dangerous waters in a small dinghy?'

Kane shrugged his shoulders. He replied: 'It would take a long time to explain. My life was in danger.'

'Yeah, we found evidence to that effect. There were several bullet holes in the side of the boat. I have to decide now what to do with you. You have placed me in a very awkward position. I have to decide whether to let the authorities know about us picking you up or . . . '

'Or what?'

The captain thought for a few seconds and then said: 'We have been having a lot of trouble lately with New Zealand fishing limits. We are not supposed to be inside their territorial waters but, of course, sometimes we do trespass, especially when the fish are running well. So was the case the other day. We picked you up inside New Zealand's waters and it so mentioned in my log. If I take you into a port there could be a lot of questions asked.'

'So you are proposing to drop me off and not mention anything to anyone, is that what you're trying to say?' asked Kane.

'That is so,' replied the captain.

'Well, it just happens that that will suit my book also.'

The captain smiled. He said: 'I thought you would understand my position. I have already arranged that you are to be dropped tonight once it gets dark.'

The Japanese captain rose from behind his desk and came around and shook Kane's hand. He said: 'Let's go out on to the bridge. We will be pulling in our nets during the next hour. You might find it interesting.'

For the remainder of that day they steamed slowly along the coast of New Zealand, sometimes in sight of land.

As soon as it was dark the Japanese fishing boat changed course. All the lights were shut off, even the navigation lamps at the bows and mast tops. Look-outs were posted around the ship and it proceeded towards land at half speed.

The captain unlocked a cabinet in the wheelhouse and brought out a revolver. He handed it to Kane with a slight grin. He said: 'Here is the revolver we found on you. It has been cleaned and oiled. Perhaps you will be needing it again.'

'Perhaps,' replied Kane, taking it and shoving it down his belt.

An hour later the captain gave the order to stop the engines and the fishing boat wallowed in the sea. Kane strained forward at the rail and could just make

148

out the land mass dead ahead. For one brief second a car's headlights could be seen.

'There is the road we were talking about,' said the captain. 'We will drop you on the beach. The dory has already been lowered.' He held out his hand.

Kane shook it and thanked him. Then he went down on to the deck and clambered over the side and down the rope ladder into the dory.

They rode the surf into the beach and Kane jumped on to the soft sand as they beached. The crew pushed the boat back into the water. Within minutes they were rowing back to the fishing boat. Kane stood on the beach watching them until they were out of sight.

He turned and walked up the beach. His eyes gradually got accustomed to the darkness and he found a pathway up a gully and followed it.

At the top of the cliff Kane found that he was on farm land. He climbed through a barbed wire fence and crossed a field almost knee deep in lush grass.

Another car went along the road, its

headlamps piercing the darkness like spotlights at a theatre. Kane judged the road at being about another two hundred yards away. He increased his stride.

After half an hour waiting on the side of the road a car came around the corner and Kane got up and stood and waved his hand.

He heard the driver change gear and put his foot on the brake. The car drew to a halt beside him. Kane moved around to the driver's side.

'Thanks for stopping,' said Kane. 'I wonder if you could give me a lift into the nearest town?'

'Yes, jump in,' said the driver. 'How come you're out here on your own?'

Kane thought quickly, then he said: 'My car's in a ditch back awhile. Came around a corner and skidded off the road. Not much damage and didn't hurt myself so there's no harm done. I'll spend the night at a hotel and then come out with a tow truck first thing in the morning.'

'That's the best thing to do. You're an Australian, aren't you?'

'Yes,' replied Kane. 'I'm on holiday

here, just driving around. Just following my nose.' Kane was amazed at how easily he could lie.

'Where were you heading?' asked the driver.

'Oh, nowhere in particular.'

'Rotorua's not far away. You ought to visit there.'

'I might do that.'

'Amazing, really, all that thermal stuff. The whole town must be delicately poised on a thin crust of earth above a steaming cauldron. Heaven knows what would happen if there was a sudden earthquake there.'

Kane nodded his head. On the seat beside him was a road map. He picked it up and held it so that he got a reflection from the light on the dashboard. After checking a few road signs he found out more or less where he was.

Kane stayed the night in a hotel in the small town where he was dropped. He ate a late dinner in a sidewalk café and then retired to his room. He was asleep as soon as his head touched the pillow.

The next morning he was up early. He

walked through the street until he came to a men's outfitters. He went in and made the owner's day by buying a complete sports outfit, a suitcase and some spare shirts.

A truck driver gave him a lift into Rotorua and dropped him outside Moore's Hotel, the one that June Belamy had mentioned.

Kane walked into the foyer and up to the desk. A young girl raised her head and smiled at Kane.

'Yes, sir?' she asked.

Kane asked for a room and was given one in the 600 block. An elderly grey-haired man picked up his suitcase and took him along the corridors to his room. Kane followed him.

'Tell me, is there a Miss Belamy staying here?' Kane asked as they reached the single room.

The porter opened the door and went in. He placed Kane's bag on the luggage rack and turned around. He scratched his head. 'Miss Belamy? The name sounds familiar. What does she look like?'

'Brunette, about five-five, on the heavy side. About thirty-five years old.'

'I know who you mean,' said the porter. 'Yes, she's in. You'll most probably find her in the Cabana Lounge. She spends most of her time in there.'

'Thanks,' said Kane, giving the man a tip.

Kane closed the door after the porter had gone and turned on the shower. He stripped and then stood underneath the stream of water. He rubbed the scented soap into his skin, letting the grime and sweat of the last few days soak out of his pores.

He dressed in his sports clothes and let himself out of the room. After studying the hotel plan he made his way along the corridors to the Cabana Lounge.

He pushed open the door and entered. He looked quickly around the room and then made his way towards the bar. As he turned a slight corner he saw June, perched on top of a leather-covered stool, holding a martini glass in her hand, studying her reflection in the mirror facing the counter.

At the sight of Kane she swung herself around and shouted: 'Why Adam, you old bastard! So you've made it! Come and have a drink!'

Kane smiled weakly and went to meet her.

'Hell, I never thought I'd see you again,' she shouted. 'This calls for a celebration. Barman, break open a bottle of champagne!'

The barman sighed a deep sigh and looked at Kane. There was a look of fatigue in his eyes. Kane guessed that June had been giving him a bad time. The barman went in search of a bottle of champagne.

11

Hell's Gate

'Then what happened?' asked Kane. 'After you docked at Auckland?'

'The captain reported the incident to the dock police,' June replied, 'and in no time the whole wharf was swarming. We were all questioned and had to make statements. An immediate search was set underway for you, but they didn't hold out much hope. They all said you were very foolish.'

'What did they have to say about the launch?' asked Kane.

'They were more interested in you. The papers invented a story that you were trying to smuggle dope or something into New Zealand and the launch belonged to a rival gang who you had double-crossed. It made exciting reading.'

Kane laughed. 'So as far as Ben Collins is concerned I'm still out in the Pacific drifting around in an open boat.'

'You seem to have a charmed life, Adam,' said June. 'All those hundreds of square miles and you happen to be in the same one as a Jap boat.'

'That's how it goes sometimes. You know, I should have known directly I was attacked at the Korulevu Hotel that Paul Smithers was the Big Boy but I just couldn't see it, it was so fantastic! The first inkling was when I saw the name on that launch. KATHREEN is his wife's name and I'd seen a photograph of the launch on his desk at his house.'

He poured out some more champagne. Then he continued: 'Paul Smithers will have received a report from Ben Collins by now. He'll think I'm dead. You are the only person who knows I'm alive and fit. I'll get back to Australia tomorrow and have it out with Paul. That's going to be the hardest part of this whole case because Paul and I are old friends.'

'They must be a big organisation, Adam,' said June. 'I mean, they hired a plane to make an extensive airsearch after they found you'd left Fiji. Then they must

156

have brought over that launch from Australia. They're spending a lot of money trying to find you.'

'A small amount, really, with what they plan to make.' Kane offered June a cigarette and then lit them both with a match. A piece of tobacco caught in between one of his teeth and he clipped off the end of the match and searched for it. June looked sideways at him.

'You reminded me just then of a particularly persistent reporter down in Auckland,' said June.

'How do you mean?'

'With that matchstick in your mouth,' June replied.

Kane put his glass down on the bar top. His whole face changed in an instant to a narrow sneer. He moved around on his bar stool and took hold of June's hand. He asked, harshly: 'What was this fellow like? Describe him to me!'

'Why, Adam, what's come over you?'

'Never mind,' replied Kane. 'Describe this man! Was he short and thin! Longish hair?'

'Yes, he was,' replied June. 'He also had

a lot of spots on the back of his neck. And, of course, a matchstick stuck between his teeth all the time. Why, do you know him?'

'I'll say I do! That was no reporter — that was Ben Collins! He must have mingled with the crowd on the wharf trying to glean some information out of you all. What did you tell him?'

'Nothing of any importance,' said June. 'What was there to tell? We didn't know where you were except that you had gone off in the dinghy. What else could we tell him?'

'I guess you couldn't have told him much,' said Kane, thoughtfully. 'What did he ask you?'

June thought for a while, taking a sip of her champagne. The barman was at the far end of the bar serving a couple of men who had just come in. Kane gave the men a quick glance and then returned his attention to June.

'I don't think I could remember the whole conversation word for word but I remember his opening statement was that I was friendly with you on the trip over.

He said that one of the other passengers had told him.'

'What did you say to that?' asked Kane.

June laughed. She said: 'I asked him what bloody business it was of his.'

'Then what?'

'He asked what you had planned doing once getting to Auckland and I told him that I thought you'd be going back to Australia as quickly as possible. I remember he nodded his head when I told him that. Oh yes, I told him that you might contact me here.'

'You told him that?' asked Kane.

'Yes, remember how we agreed you'd contact me once you made a landfall just to let me know you were all right. Why, have I done the wrong thing?'

'I don't know,' Kane replied. 'I don't know.'

He was silent for a few seconds. He thought that maybe it wasn't too healthy having Ben Collins know that he was planning on coming down to Rotorua after landing. But then certain developments had changed the whole picture. As far as Ben was concerned he, Kane, was still missing.

'Come on,' said Kane. 'Let's finish this bottle and then have some lunch.'

They both waved to the barman as they left the bar.

It was while having lunch that they heard of Hell's Gate for the first time. Their waitress was a mine of information.

'Most people who come here go out to Whakarewarewa, which is just a short bus ride out,' she said. 'They rave about it, but they've seen nothing really. Hell's Gate is the place to go.'

'Hell's Gate! Sounds good,' said June. 'Does it live up to its name?'

'I'll say it does,' the waitress replied. 'It's not far, about ten miles out.'

'How about it, June?' asked Kane. 'We'll go out there this afternoon and have a look at it.'

'You won't regret it,' said the waitress. 'It never fails to fascinate me.'

After lunch Kane went to the hotel office and arranged to hire a car for the afternoon. The receptionist fixed up all the necessary papers and then handed him a set of keys. He smiled his thanks and went to meet June.

They reached the turn-off to Hell's Gate inside half an hour. In front of them was a mass of steam and smoke, looking as if the whole area was a smouldering cauldron, ready to explode at any moment. Kane stopped the car and switched off the engine.

'Well,' he said. 'Here we are.'

'Adam, I'm rather frightened,' June said. 'I wasn't expecting anything like this. It's terrifying!'

'Come on, June,' said Kane, getting out of the car. 'This is happening all the time. There's nothing to be afraid of.'

'No. I think I'll stay in the car. You go and have a look around. It's too scary for me!'

Kane shrugged his shoulders and wandered off down the path. He followed it slowly, walking towards the clouds of steam and sulphurous gases which enveloped the area. The pathway ran along the side of a cliff. Kane looked over the railings at the boiling brown mud pools below him.

A jet of boiling water suddenly shot up in a geyser a hundred yards in front of him. The roar reached his ears seconds later. The water hung in the air and then cascaded down in a thunderous roar. It was a sight well worth seeing.

Kane followed the pathway as it spiralled down to the hot mud pools. He stood near the edge of one and watched the mud popping and gurgling like, he imagined, a vat of hot chocolate at a sweet factory. He stood watching it, fascinated, for several seconds.

He wandered slowly around Hell's Gate for half an hour, absolutely absorbed in the incredible wonders of nature at its best. When he had seen enough he started to climb the pathway leading out of the thermal area.

He was half-way up the steep pathway when he realised that a man was watching him from above. A curious shiver ran down his spine, a shiver which he had experienced numerous occasions before; one which told him that danger was close.

He stopped and looked up at the man, shielding his eyes with his hand. The man was standing so that only his silhouette was visible. His features were hidden in dark shade. But the man's outline was enough to go by. It was that of Ben Collins.

Kane turned his head and studied the landscape. The thermal area covered all the ground below him. There was only one way out and that was up the pathway he was on. Kane looked up the hill again and saw that Ben was moving slowly down the pathway towards him. He was holding a knife in his left hand, just letting it hang so that it brushed his trouser leg.

Kane felt a sudden chill in the wind as the spray from one of the many geysers swept over the pathway. He shivered and turned around. He knew he was at a disadvantage being on a level below Ben.

He quickly walked down the pathway, searching furtively for a way out. He remembered the sign board he'd read on entering the thermal area and the warning it had given about straying off the pathway.

He turned a bend and looked behind him. Ben Collins was closing the gap quickly. He was about thirty yards away.

Kane could see the sadistic smile on his face, punctuated by the matchstick stuck between his teeth.

The pathway led along a shoulder with a steep drop on the right side. To the left was thick bush hanging precariously to the volcanic soil. Kane tried to climb the steep bank in an effort to get back to the car, but the bushes which he held on to came away by the roots from the crumbling soil. The chances of him climbing the bank faded. He caught a glimpse of Ben turning the bend of the pathway out of the corner of his eye. He started running down the pathway towards the mud pools.

And then he saw the cunning of the people he was up against. Ahead of him with a revolver in his hand, was Kordina. He was standing with his feet straddling the pathway. As he saw Kane turn the corner he raised the revolver to waist height and pointed the barrel at Kane's stomach.

Kane instinctively threw himself to the ground and rolled over. The bullet smacked into the dust beside his face, almost blinding him. He rolled over again and went underneath the railings and over the side of the steep cliff.

The mud pools at the bottom of the drop were bubbling and spitting. Kane dug his fingers into the loose volcanic soil. Somehow he found a firm rock and managed to stop himself from toppling in.

Kordina looked over the cliff, saw Kane getting to his feet and raised the gun. He couldn't miss from the range he was at. Kane looked both ways and saw that his only chance was to go along the edge of the mud pools, but even as he started off he was bracing himself for the shot which would tear into his body at any second.

He heard a shout above him and glanced back to see Ben Collins holding Kordina's arm and shaking his head.

Kane ran along the edge of the pool until he could go no further. His narrow pathway to freedom was completely cut off. The volcanic slope and the mud pools joined without any solid earth between them. Kane turned around looking for another way out. He could see that Ben was sliding down the slope.

Then he saw it, but his heart skipped a beat when he saw how narrow it was and what it was surrounded by. Between two of the mud pools was a narrow strip of encrusted mud. It was either that or face up to Ben Collins and his knife.

Ben trod carefully along the edge of the mud pools, choosing his footing with precise steps. Not once did his eyes move off Kane. The knife was held steady in his left hand, the tip glistening in the sun.

Kane knew he had two alternatives. Either stay and have it out with Ben or try and walk between the mud pools to the other side. A quick glance up the cliff made Kane's mind up for him as he saw the glint of Kordina's revolver.

When Ben Collins was less than five yards away, Kane made his move. He darted along the narrow crust of mud and then jumped to the safety of a rock. A sudden belch from the pool caused a blinding cloud of steam to rise behind him.

Kane saw Ben balancing himself on the crust of mud and begin inching his way across the gap. He was half-way across when another cloud of steam belched out. Kane watched as Ben Collins over-balanced and tried to regain it by waving his arms. With a curious gurgle the crust of mud gave way and in a hiss of steam he disappeared into the boiling mud which took the place of the narrow bridge.

It was over so suddenly that Kane didn't realise for a few seconds what had happened. It was as if a magician had waved his magic wand and made Ben disappear in a cloud of smoke.

A shot and a sharp pain in his left arm made Kane come to his senses. Through the steam he could see Kordina aiming his next shot. He was using his forearm as a rest. Kane turned and jumped as the man pressed the trigger. The bullet tore through his shirt, grazing his back.

Kane managed to clear a small mud pool and land on firm ground again. Holding his left arm he quickly scrambled to the top of a bank and threw himself over. Another shot whistled past his ear.

He got to his feet and started running. He ran parallel to the mud pools, keeping behind the protective bank out of sight of Kordina. He passed a geyser, which was spouting boiling water. He was so close to the mouth of it that the spray scalded his face and hands.

Blood from the wound in his left arm began to seep out through the tear in his jacket. He felt the wound gingerly with his right hand, found that it wasn't an artery, and then started making his way towards where he had left June and the car.

He stumbled the last few yards and went to open the door, but before he could get to it he heard June call out. 'Adam, Adam. Get in the other side, quick!'

Kane went around the car and got in the open door. He slid along the seat and slammed the door shut. He looked up at June and forced a smile. 'Am I glad to see you,' he said.

June slammed her foot down on the accelerator. 'I heard the shooting and saw those two men after you,' she said. 'One of them was that reporter fellow who questioned me in Auckland.'

June looked sideways at Kane as she swung the wheel to get on the main road back to Rotorua. She saw the blood on his sports jacket for the first time. 'Hey, Adam,' she cried. 'You've been hurt!'

Kane twisted his head to look at her. He said: 'You don't say.' He smiled briefly and then slumped forward on to the dashboard.

12

A Coincidence

Kane opened his eyes and stared at the ceiling. A sudden movement in the room made him jerk his head around. A pain shot through his left arm and he let out a cry.

June moved quickly to his side and placed a hand on his forehead. She said, softly: 'Everything's all right, Adam. Just lie still and take it easy.'

'Who's in the room with you?' Kane asked, settling his head back on to the pillow.

'The barman from Moore's. Brian Newman. He's been a great help.'

The barman came over to the bedside and looked down at Kane. 'How about a brandy?' he asked. 'Might make you feel better.'

Kane nodded his head. June sat down beside him on the bed and said: 'I guess you'll want to know what's been going on?'

Kane nodded his head again and took hold of the drink which Brian brought over. He sat up and took a sip of the brandy. 'Where am I, for a start?' he asked.

'We're at Brian's flat,' said June. 'Luckily, I caught him just as he was about to finish his stint at the bar. I told him you were in trouble; that you'd been shot in the arm and were out in the car . . . '

'I said the best place to take you would be the hospital,' Brian said. 'But June seemed to hang back on that suggestion so I knew there was another side to the story. I suggested you came back here. I've looked at your arm, the bullet went clean through the flesh without touching the bone. Another quarter of an inch and it would have been a different story.'

'Brian was a medical student for several years,' said June. 'So you've been properly looked after.'

'June told me a bit about what's been going on; about the yacht and the

Japanese fishing boat picking you up. I see from a card in your wallet that you're an investigator from an Australian Insurance Company, so I figured maybe it's got something to do with some job you're working on.'

'You figured right,' said Kane. 'And I'm very grateful to you. The whole story would take a lot of telling but the gist is that these people are trying to stop me from getting back to Australia and putting a stop to a million dollar swindle.'

Brian whisled between his teeth. 'A million, eh? No wonder they're in a shooting mood!'

'One of them is no longer with us,' said Kane. He told them about how Ben Collins had chased him down into the mud-pools and how the narrow bridge of encrusted mud had collapsed on him.

'I've got to get back to Australia in the next few days to stop this thing,' Kane continued, 'I've got to get out of Rotorua somehow without being seen. There's still one of them around and he won't leave any stone unturned until he finds me. It will also be dangerous for you, June. They most probably saw us together.'

'I'll go out and have a look around town,' said Brian. 'I'll keep my ears and eyes open and try to pick up some information.'

'Thanks, Brian,' said Kane. 'Before you go, though, tell me how I could get out of Rotorua and back to Australia. What would be the quickest way?'

'Fly out,' replied Brian. 'Look, I'll go into the bar later tonight. Two of the airline boys get in there every night. I'll have a talk with them. Maybe they can fix up something.'

Kane got off the bed after Brian had left and he walked slowly around the flat. 'That was a bit of quick thinking on your part, taking Brian into your confidence,' Kane said.

'It was either that or take you to hospital,' June said. 'I thought that if the hospital authorities saw that bullet wound they'd call in the police.'

'And they'd connect it with the shooting at Hell's Gate. Someone's bound to have heard it.'

June said: 'The two men walked past

the car and I recognised one of them. It was the small, thin one; the one that I thought was a reporter up at Auckland. Directly I saw him I knew something was up so I followed them down the path. They split and the taller one made his way around the hill, then the thin man took out a knife and carried on down the path. There was no way I could warn you, Adam. I saw them closing in on you and saw you trying to make your way across those mud-pools. I thought the best thing was to have the car ready to go. It was all I could do in the circumstances.'

'You did the right thing, June. There wasn't much else you could have done.'

Brian came back just after eleven. 'You should have heard everyone talking in the bar tonight,' he began. 'You'd have thought the Third World War had started!'

'What were they saying?' asked June.

'From what I could make out,' said Brian, pouring himself out a drink. 'An elderly American couple saw the whole episode; the chase, the shooting and that fellow being swallowed up in the mud-pools. They reported it to the police. So did another bunch of tourists. They told them they had seen a man running up the path with his arm practically severed off. That must have been you, Kane.'

'Was there any mention of June?' asked Kane.

'No. But the police were nosing around the office at the hotel having a look at the register. They also searched your room and found your revolver under the pillow. I think they've tied you up into this mystery.'

'Did you manage to see those airline boys?' Kane asked.

Brian lit a cigarette. He said: 'Yes, they came in around ten. I managed to get them to one side after a while. I told them you were a businessman from Auckland down here for a bit of fun on the sly but then found that a detective agency, hired by your wife, was on your tail. I said you wanted to get back to Auckland by some method other than car or regular flight. I told them the airport and your car were being watched.'

June laughed. She said: 'You can sure spin a story.'

'So what did they say?' asked Kane.

'They might be able to help,' replied Brian. 'They're going to phone me later tonight. Apparently there's a fellow down here with his own plane who's flying back to Auckland at five in the morning. They're going to contact him and see if he'll take you both back.'

'That's fine,' said Kane. 'Then I could catch the next flight out to Sydney. With any luck I could be back tomorrow night.'

'Am I to come with you?' asked June.

Kane turned and looked at her. 'I think it would be better if you did, June. If Kordina's still hanging around and sees you he'll go to any length to get information out of you. I think the wisest choice would be to leave everything here and come back with me to Auckland. You can always write the hotel and have your things sent on.'

'I agree,' said Brian. 'If they're out to kill Kane they wouldn't stop just because you were holding back information.'

'Thanks! You've just made up my mind for me!' June replied.

'So that's settled,' said Kane. 'Now all

we're waiting for is confirmation.' He looked at his watch and saw that it was nearly twelve.

Brian put on some records and then had another look at Kane's arm. The wound was clean, although a bit ragged around the edges.

The phone rang at five minutes to two. Brian got up from the settee and answered it. He looked at Kane during the conversation and nodded his head. The flight was on!

★   ★   ★

It was raining in Auckland when the Cessna landed. Kane bundled June into a taxi, after he had squared the pilot for the trip, and he told the driver to take them to a hotel which wouldn't ask them questions about not having any luggage.

The driver nodded his head and said he knew of one which was on the waterfront; that he also knew the proprietor. The driver looked in the rearview mirror at June, shrugged his shoulders and let out the clutch.

'When are you going to fly back to Sydney?' June asked.

'Tonight! I'll contact the airline office directly we get to the hotel and try and get a seat on tonight's flight,' Kane answered. 'What are you going to do?'

'I don't know. I think I'll go back to the yacht and see when they're due to sail again. I can see you're in a hurry to get back. Maybe I might get in the way if I stay around.'

'I wouldn't say that, June. You've been a tremendous help to me. It's a pity we couldn't have met under different circumstances. But I am in a hurry. I must get moving.'

'So it's going to be 'goodbye' then?' asked June, looking straight ahead.

Kane nodded his head. 'Maybe we'll meet again, sometime.'

'Maybe,' replied June, with just a trace of a tear forming in the corner of her eye. 'Maybe!'

★   ★   ★

Kane stayed under the hot jet until the water began to get cool. Afterwards he dried himself slowly, only patting around the wound with the towel. He took another look underneath the bandage and decided the inflammation had definitely gone down.

He wrapped the thick towel around his waist and walked out into the bedroom. He sat down on the edge of the bed and lit a cigarette. He thought that dropping June at the wharf where the yacht was moored had been a good thing. Not that he had wanted to get rid of her, for he hadn't, but it was wiser that she had nothing else to do with him just in case the organisation moved in. And she had understood, which had been a great help. Maybe, Kane thought, the little episode at Hell's Gate had taught her that Kane's life expectancy wasn't all that bright. Maybe she had seen the light!

He looked around for the telephone, saw that it was on top of the bookcase behind the head of the bed. He picked up the receiver and dialled 'O' and waited for the receptionist to answer.

'This is Kane from Room 17,' he told

the girl. 'Would you put me through to Tolls please.'

When the operator came on the line he asked for a Sydney number. The operator told him to hold the line while she connected him. After three minutes she told him to go ahead.

'Jim, this is Adam Kane speaking. I'm in Auckland, New Zealand of all places. How's things over in Aussie?'

Kane smiled at the reply he got. He continued: 'Look, Jim, I'm in a spot of trouble over a case I've been working on and I'd like you to be in your office between eleven and twelve tonight. I'll be on tonight's flight.'

Jim Brady said he would be there.

'Good,' Kane said. 'Have a bottle open. I'm going to need it. See you Jim.' He replaced the receiver into its cradle.

Kane looked at his watch and saw that he had four hours to wait until he was due at the airport. Suddenly he felt tired and he rang down to the receptionist and told her to wake him at five. He got between the sheets and closed his eyes. He was asleep inside two minutes.

Kane checked in at Air New Zealand and the clerk referred to the passenger list and checked Kane's name off with his pen. When the flight was announced Kane was one of the first to leave. He walked through the numbered doorway out to the tarmac. A ground hostess checked his ticket and told him which way to go. Kane walked along the white indicating line towards the front of the DC8 and climbed the steps. A steward showed him to his seat. He was pleased to see that he had been given a window seat.

The other passengers began to arrive and Kane looked at the first two or three and then settled down in his seat looking for his seat belt. He had a hard time finding the left strap but in the end managed to secure it around his waist. By the time he had fastened it the jet was ready for take-off. The flight was only half filled and nobody had been placed next to him.

In minutes they were airborne.

Kane watched the lights disappearing

beneath them and then, when they were no longer visible, turned his attention to the lighted sign above the door. He suddenly realised that he wanted a cigarette.

As he was watching, the lights on the board were switched out and the stewardess announced over the intercom that the passengers could smoke if they wanted to and that drinks would be available.

Kane searched in his pocket and got out his packet of cigarettes. He took one out and put it in his mouth. His matches were in his left hand jacket pocket and he drew his right arm across his body to get them out. He found that he couldn't quite reach them.

A hand came through the back of the seat, in between the gap. It was a man's hand and it held a gold-plated Ronson lighter. The thumb pressed down on the flick-top and a small gas flame appeared. 'Allow me,' said the man.

Kane bent sideways and touched the end of his cigarette to the flame. He drew in and lighted the cigarette. 'Thanks a lot,' said Kane, looking around.

The lighter was quickly withdrawn and then the man's hand came through the gap in the seat again. This time it held a snub-nosed .38 revolver, which was pointing at Kane's mid-section. The man whispered through the gap: 'This, believe it or not, Kane, is a coincidence. I didn't know you would be on this plane, but seeing that you are, I think I'll come and sit next to you. Just one thing, make a move and I'll have you right here. I've got nothing to lose.'

Kane looked up at the man as he rose from his seat. It was Kordina!

13

'What a Way to Go!'

Kordina dug his elbow into Kane's side.

Kane awoke with a start. He looked sideways at Kordina and then at the hand stuck inside the coat holding the revolver. He leant back and closed his eyes again.

'For crissakes wake up! You're putting me on edge!' said Kordina. 'How the hell can you go to sleep at a time like this?'

'Maybe I'm not sleeping,' said Kane, out of the corner of his mouth. 'Maybe I'm thinking.'

'Yeah! Well, thinking's not going to do you much good. I've got this friend meeting me off the plane and then we're going to take you up to The Gap. They say it's a long drop down on to the rocks.'

Kane adjusted his seat to the upright position and looked out of the window. His reflection stared back at him. He felt his wound with his right hand. It wasn't as painful as before. He moved his arm in a circular motion, testing it.

'I should have got you with that shot. Seeing Ben disappear put me off.'

Kane laughed. He said: 'Poor old Ben. He should have watched his step.'

'Yeah,' said Kordina, philosophically. 'You can't win all the time! He had a run of bad luck with you. We were talking it over one night after you got away from us at Korulevu. He told me that you were the first person he'd missed. It irked him. It preyed on his mind. Maybe that's why he never got you, maybe he talked himself out of it.'

'Maybe,' said Kane. He watched the stewardess as she walked by carrying a couple of drinks on a tray. He wondered what she'd do if she knew there was a frightened gunman on board.

For that's what Kordina was, thought Kane. Frightened. It stood out like a sore thumb. He worked for the organisation and the Big Boy and they didn't like failures. And Kordina had failed, just as Ben Collins had. It had only been a stroke of luck that Kordina had boarded the same flight as himself.

If they hadn't been on the same flight then Kordina would have been going back to Australia without having fulfilled his mission. And, so Kane told himself, that was like signing his own death warrant.

Kane knew that he was up against it, that maybe the cards were stacked too high against him. Kordina was so eager to kill him to get back into the Big Boy's favour that anything could happen, witnesses or not. That's why he had played it cool, not for his own safety but for the other passengers. If a bullet pierced the fuselage at the height they were flying then the whole lot of them would be killed. Kane closed his eyes at the thought.

Kordina looked at his wristwatch and said: 'We'll be there inside half an hour. My advice to you is to take it easy. Just do as I say. Okay?'

Kane nodded his head. He thought that to try to contact the captain or one of the stewards and to try and overpower Kordina was out of the question. The

186

alternative would have to be at Sydney when they landed. Somehow, while crossing the tarmac or going through Customs, he'd have to make a break for it. It was a wild idea but it was the only one he'd been able to think of during the flight.

The plane touched down with only the slightest bump and then the jets were reversed. Kane looked out of the window at the runway lights which were flashing past. Then the terminal buildings came into view and he could see the white-uniformed ground crew busying themselves with the ramps and refuelling pumps.

The giant jet swung around off the runway and slowly made its way to a position in front of the main building. Kane could see the crowds lining the top of the building eagerly scanning the windows of the jet. He wondered which one amongst them was Kordina's friend.

The jet stopped and the doors were opened and a gust of fresh air came through the fuselage. Kane undid his seat-belt and waited for Kordina to make a move. He noticed that he was letting everyone else off first so that the tarmac wouldn't be crowded. He was definitely playing things safe.

Kane looked about him as he walked across the tarmac towards the doors leading to the Customs halls. The last passenger was just entering the doorway about twenty yards in front of them. Kane looked to the left of the building. There was a wire fence about four feet high surrounding an out-of-bounds area. Kane thought about making a run for it but decided it was too much in the open to stand a chance. A bullet would hit him before he reached the wire fence.

'In you go, Kane, and remember I'm right behind you,' said Kordina. 'Just answer the man's questions as if nothing was happening.'

Kane swung open the door and went through. He joined on the end of the queue of passengers waiting for their turn at the long benches. Kane watched the door which they went through after they had passed the Custom's examination.

The officer looked through Kordina's overnight bag and then stuck the clearance tape on the outside and waved him through. Kane walked ahead and opened the door.

Leaning against the railing about twenty yards away was Jim Brady. He was smoking a cigarette inserted into a white ivory holder which was clamped firmly between his teeth. As Kane came through the door Jim pushed himself away from the post.

Kane had to act quickly. In a flash he realised the situation which would ensue if Jim came over and slapped him on the back. Kordina would have no hesitation except to gun them both down where they stood.

Kane held his finger up to his mouth, like a father does to a child when he wants him to be silent, and moved his eyes to indicate the man behind him.

Jim Brady cottoned on fast. He had been brought up in a tough school. Since doing odd jobs for Kane he had come to expect the unexpected at any time. Instead of walking towards Kane he moved at a tangent and went through the door they had just come out of. He didn't look sideways at them or give any indication that he knew them. The door swung shut behind him.

Kane and Kordina walked about ten paces further on and then Kordina told him to stop. He still held his hand in his right jacket pocket. He said: 'So far so good.'

Kane took out his cigarettes and took his time extracting one. He put it in his mouth and lit it with a match. He let the match burn near his face for several seconds so that Jim Brady would be able to recognise him in the darkness. He knew that Jim would play it safe; that he wouldn't be too far behind. Kane was ready for when the action started. He stood on the balls of his feet, perfectly poised, like a leopard ready to jump.

Out of the shadows a man approached them. He stopped several yards away from them and then came forward. Kane looked the man over. He was dressed in an open-necked sports shirt. The man's chin was covered in a couple of days stubble and his hair, which was a dirty grey colour, was dishevelled.

190

'Hi, there, Kordina,' he said. 'Who's this guy with you?'

'You'll never guess, Hans. This is the celebrated Mr. Adam Kane who the late Ben Collins and I have been chasing all over the Pacific.'

'But I thought you said over the phone that you'd . . . '

'Yeah, I had lost him for a while but then I picked up the trail again and managed to jump him as he boarded the plane. You can forget about me going into hiding, Hans. I'll be all right now with the organisation.'

'I'll say,' replied Hans. 'This should make the Big Boy happy. I hear through the grapevine that they're planning to pull out of the deal seeing that this guy's still on the loose. I guess now they can go ahead with it?'

'Yep. I'm going to enjoy the moment when I report personally to the Big Boy and tell him that Kane's dead.'

'I'll say! Now what?'

'You've got my car here some place?' Kordina asked.

The man nodded his head. He said:

'It's over in the car park. What do you plan doing with this Kane guy? The quicker he's got out of the way, the better. He's given us a lot of trouble.'

'Let's start walking,' said Kordina. 'I'll tell you what we're going to do as we go. Okay, Kane, start walking towards those parked cars and remember, there's two guns on you now. You're taking your last walk, my friend.'

Kane cleared his throat and spat on the ground. He looked first at Kordina and then at the man called Hans. He said: 'I'd like about five minutes with each of you, alone and without those guns of yours. I'd beat you into a pulp. You're nothing once those guns have been taken away from you. Nothing but a couple of yellow-bellied punks.'

'Steady, Kane. Steady,' said Kordina. 'We don't want to make a mess of the tarmac.'

Hans took out a revolver from under his left arm and stuck it in Kane's rib. He said: 'Walk, bastard. Walk.'

Kane started walking slowly towards the parked cars. He looked to the left and

192

right trying to pinpoint Jim Brady. He knew that somewhere, out there in the rim of darkness, his friend was watching, watching and waiting to pounce.

'Put your gun away, Hans,' said Kordina. 'We don't want anyone seeing this guy with a gun stuck in his back.'

Kane came to the rows of parked cars and turned his head around to get a direction from the two men. Hans pointed down the next column and said: 'It's the eighth one down that row.'

They walked in between the cars. The lights from the Terminal building were hardly visible and it was hard to see where they were going. There were about twenty cars parked in a line and Kane quickly counted up to the eighth one and then judged the distance. He thought he'd try and duck behind it when he came to it on the off chance that Jim was around. Kane knew that to get into the car would be fatal. Once inside they'd have a gun sticking in his ribs until the moment they pushed him over the cliff.

They were passing the fourth car when

another car pulled out ahead of them and switched on its headlights. It reversed into the space between the two rows of cars and then started moving towards them. Kane kept walking in the centre of the tarmac. He was peering hard into the bright lights, trying to see the nameplate of the car.

Judging by the space of the headlights he thought it was an American car. Jim Brady drove around in a right-hand drive Dodge. The car started accelerating and then the left-hand indicator light started flashing. Kane quickly made a decision. If he was wrong he'd be dead, but it was a hunch worth taking.

The car came straight at them and Kane quickly glanced over his shoulder at the two gunmen. They were moving over to the left-hand side of the tarmac so as to let the car pass. Kane noticed that they had both put their guns into their coat pockets. They hadn't realised that there was the possibility of the car being directed at them.

Kane began moving over to the left-hand side and then, when the car was about five yards away, suddenly dived across the tarmac so that the car would be between him and the gunmen. He heard Kordina swear but the squeal of brakes drowned out anything further.

Kane picked himself up and started running, making sure that the car was between him and Kordina and Hans. The car slowed down and then the left-hand door flew open. Kane judged the distance and jumped for the opening. He winced as he had to use his left arm to hold on to the frame, but he made it with inches to spare. He pulled himself along the leather seat, keeping his head down below the level of the back window. He slammed the door shut, looked up at Jim Brady, who was crouched over the steering wheel with a smile over his entire face and the absurd ivory cigarette holder clamped between his teeth, and yelled: 'Thanks Jim. Now get the hell out of here!'

'Keep your head down, old boy. I think things are going to warm up a bit.'

He had just finished speaking when they heard a shot fired and felt the thud as the bullet hit the bodywork of the car.

They heard two other shots but neither of them found the car. Jim Brady swung the wheel and accelerated across the wide, empty space with the tyres screaming in protest.

Kane turned and looked out of the rear window. At first there was no sign of a car following but soon a pair of headlights appeared from the other end of the parking lot. He saw that Kordina and Hans were trying to cut them off. They were at least three hundred yards away.

'Where to, sport?' asked Jim Brady, swinging the wheel and swerving around an island.

'You know the roads around here, Jim. Just lose that car and you'll have done a good night's work!'

'That shouldn't be hard. You'll find some cigarettes in the glove compartment. Hand me one over.'

'I'll never be able to understand you, Jim. Here we are being chased by a couple of killers and all you're interested in is having a cigarette!' Kane reached into the compartment and took out the open packet of Lucky Strikes and shook one out. He lit it and handed it over to Jim.

'Thanks,' said Jim, glancing in the rearview mirror and then swinging the wheel hard to the right. He fumbled around with the ivory holder and inserted the cigarette.

Kane felt the wound on his left arm and noticed that it was bleeding. He took out his handkerchief and stuffed it down the arm of his coat. He turned and looked out of the window again and saw a car swinging around the corner. He judged that they had gained a hundred yards.

'Can't you get a little more out of her, Jim?' asked Kane.

'Sure can, but we're going to get into heavy traffic soon. We'll lose them quickly once we do.'

Jim Brady went through a red light and turned the corner into one of the main thoroughfares leading into the heart of the city. He pulled over to the outside lane of traffic and then gunned the motor. The car leapt forward and the speedometer registered eighty-two miles an hour.

'That's more like it,' said Kane. He

looked out of the rear window and had the surprise of his life. The car following them had caught up and was trailing them less than a hundred yards away.

'They're right behind us!' exclaimed Kane.

'Hell! They must have a souped-up motor in that thing. Hold on, here we go!'

Without any warning and without signals, Jim Brady swung the wheel and broadsided around a corner. They narrowly missed a truck coming in the opposite direction.

Jim Brady corrected the slide and weaved in and out of the traffic in front. Kane continued looking out of the rear window and saw the other car slowly catching up with them.

'Jim, I hate to say this again, but those guys are pulling us in! They'll be in shooting distance soon!' Kane looked sideways at his friend and saw the small beads of perspiration forming on his forehead.

'I'm doing my best, old sport, but that fellow driving knows his business. What's your plan?'

'I haven't one,' said Kane, closing his

eyes as the car overtook a slow Austin on the blind side. 'I hadn't thought about you meeting me.'

'That was a piece of luck, wasn't it?' said Jim. 'I had nothing to do so I thought I'd surprise you. Some surprise, eh?'

'Have you got your revolver with you?' asked Kane, urgently, as he saw the other car closing up the gap.

'No, the police took it away from me after that rumpus two months ago. I haven't got a thing.'

Ahead of them was a roundabout and three cars were stopped, giving way to the traffic on their right. Jim Brady had no alternative except to slow down and mount the pavement to pass them. Several of the cars sounded their horns and one moved forward, giving the car behind them space to pass through.

'They're right on top of us, Jim. We'll have to do something drastic. I think the best thing is for you to stop and let me out the next chance you get. I'll stand a better chance on my own. I don't want you getting yourself further involved in my problems.'

'Forget it, Adam,' said Jim, practically standing on the accelerator. 'I told you I'd lose them. I'm going to do a U-turn at the next corner, so hold on to your seat.'

Kane studied the car following them. It was less than twenty yards away and he wondered why they hadn't fired at them before now. He could make out Kordina's face every time they went past a lamp standard and saw that he was looking down at his hands beneath the dashboard. He imagined that he was checking or reloading his revolver.

The distance between them lessened to ten yards and then they were drawing beside them. Jim Brady looked out of the open window and said to Kane: 'This is it, old sport. I'm going to brake and then swing this wheel hard. I might not make it so get ready to jump. See you later!'

Kane saw Jim move his hands around the wheel and at the same moment saw Kordina put his hand out of the window and throw an object at them. The oval-shaped object hit the steering wheel and then ran along the top of the dashboard before falling on to the floor of the car, but in that time, which was only a split second, both Jim and Kane had recognised it.

'A hand-grenade!' shouted Jim.

'Jump out, Jim!' yelled Kane. 'Jump!' He opened his door and threw himself out into the darkness.

Jim let go of the steering wheel and pulled down on the inside handle but the lock was on. In desperation he flung himself across the front seat and tried to follow Kane out of the open door. There was a sudden flash of light and the car exploded into a thousand pieces.

Kordina turned around in his seat, and told Hans to slow down. He said: 'That's the end of Mister Bloody Kane and his friend. Now let's get out of this area. We've done enough for one night.'

'What a way to go!' said Hans to himself. 'What a way to go!'

14

No Way Out

The ambulance arrived at the same time as the two police cars. The crowd, which had quickly formed around the wrecked car, fell back as the ambulance inched its way slowly towards Jim Brady, who was hanging half-in and half-out of the near-side door.

The police formed a ring around the car and asked the crowd to fall back so as to give the ambulance men enough room to work. The senior police officer got out his notebook, and together with a constable, started questioning the onlookers.

One of the ambulance men looked up and shook his head. He said: 'There's nothing we can do. He's dead!'

The officer came over: 'This doesn't look like an ordinary accident to me. How badly is the fellow knocked about?

Three people living in this street say they heard an explosion.'

'You can see for yourself,' replied the ambulance man. 'He's been burnt and there's metal embedded down one side of him.'

'A bomb, eh? Sounds like gang warfare.'

'What shall we do?' the ambulance man asked.

'Don't move him yet,' replied the police officer. 'I'm having our photographer and crime squad come down.' He turned and went back to questioning the crowd.

A siren could be heard in the distance and then another police car drew up. A photographer stepped out and reported to the police officer and then went around taking shots of the car from different angles.

Two newspaper reporters arrived on the scene and soon the night was being shattered by the explosions of flashbulbs.

★   ★   ★

Kane moved an arm and felt the wet dew on the grass. He opened his eyes and saw that his head was about six inches from the base of a concrete pillar. He rolled over on to his back and stared up into the dark sky. He could hear, in the distance, a high-pitched whine.

The whine got closer and then it dawned on him; it was an ambulance. Then it came back to him; the chase through the streets of Sydney, the hand-grenade being thrown and his headlong dive out of the speeding car.

Kane put his elbows on to the soft ground and levered himself up into a sitting position. He moved slowly for fear that he might have cracked some ribs in the fall. He saw the marks on the grass verge where he had landed and skidded after diving out of the car.

A police car went past with its siren blaring and slid to a halt about sixty yards further up the road. Kane turned his head and saw, for the first time, the crowd which had gathered around the wrecked Dodge.

He put out his hand and grasped hold of the concrete pillar and pulled himself up on to his feet. A feeling of nausea passed over him and he thought he was going to pass out again. He breathed in deeply to try to clear his head.

Opposite him, on the other side of the road, was a phone booth. He staggered over to it. He thought he would ring the Sydney office and get one of the night staff to come out and collect him. Half-way across the road he decided not to. For all he knew, the organisation might have their people working throughout the West Pacific Insurance Company.

Kane thumbed through the telephone book and looked up the McClelland's number. Most of the people he knew in Sydney were associated with his firm in one way or another, and there was that feeling gnawing away at the back of his mind that he couldn't trust any of them until the case was cleaned up.

Kane heard the dialling tone and then the receiver being lifted.

An American voice answered. It was Elaine. Kane said 'Elaine, this is Adam Kane ringing.'

There was a few seconds pause and then Kane heard Elaine suck in her breath. Then she said: 'Adam, Adam, where are you? I've been so worried about you! We read in the papers that you had been lost overboard from a yacht. Where are you?'

'I'm in Sydney,' replied Kane. 'And I need your help. I've been in a car accident. Right now I would like you to come and pick me up. Has McClelland got a car?'

'Yes, he has,' replied Elaine. 'They've gone away for a couple of days and left me with it. Look, give me the address you're at and I'll come out and get you.'

Kane looked out of the phone booth at the lamp standard opposite. Half-way up, just underneath the light, was a road sign. He gave her the name of the street.

She said: 'You stay right where you are, Adam. I'll be there as soon as I can.'

He leant back against the window and tried to relax. Just as he was getting comfortable, a man came running down the road and stopped outside the phone booth. He was jingling some change in his hand and Kane noticed that he had a camera and flash attachment slung around his neck.

'Thanks, matey,' said the reporter as Kane left the phone booth. 'Must get this into the news room at once. Hell, what a story! The police reckon a hand-grenade exploded in the car. You should have seen what was left of the bloke driving it. I've never seen such a bloody mess!'

Kane grunted and walked away. He made a wall surrounding a garden and sat down. He looked back at the phone booth and saw the reporter dialling a number. Then he heard him speaking over the phone. The door had stayed open and Kane managed to hear most of the conversation. He could feel his blood rising at the description of Jim Brady's body and made a vow that both Kordina and Hans would pay for what they had done.

The reporter left the phone booth and ran back up the road to where the tow truck was inching its way through the crowd with the wrecked car behind it. The reporter started taking shots as it was being towed away.

Kane went back into the phone booth.

Jim Brady, Kane reflected, had been a good friend, one that would turn a hand to help without a moment's hesitation. He was the kind of man that thrived on adventure with no questions asked. Perhaps, thought Kane, he had been born in the wrong century. They had had good times together; exciting times, and now they were to be no more.

A car pulled to a halt opposite the phone booth and Kane peered out to see who it was. He opened the phone booth door at the same time as Elaine reached it. She stopped when she caught sight of him and quickly looked him up and down, taking in the grass-stained trousers where he had landed after diving out of the car, to his blood spattered jacket.

'Adam!' she cried. 'Whatever's happened to you!'

'Oh God, I feel bad,' said Kane, as she closed the door. 'I'm going to be a bit of a nuisance to you, Elaine. My whole inside's been shook up.'

'You're no nuisance,' said Elaine. 'We'll be home in a few minutes. What you need is a stiff brandy.'

Kane closed his eyes as she drove. His head was throbbing and his arm hurt like hell. He knew he was on his last legs; that he couldn't go on much longer.

Elaine slowed down and drove the car between the gate posts of the large two-storied house. She drove around the narrow drive until she was opposite the front door.

Once inside the house, she helped him into a big leather chair and then stood back and looked at him. She saw that his face was a deathly white and that his left arm was bleeding. She rushed outside and closed the front door and then went into the kitchen and filled up the electric jug for some hot water. She searched around for the first-aid kit.

When she returned into the living-room she found that Kane had passed out. He had fallen sideways and was leaning over one arm of the chair.

As she lifted his arm to take off his jacket he opened his eyes and moaned and she dropped it for fear that she was hurting him. He mumbled some words but she didn't manage to catch what he said. She tried to get his left arm out of the jacket.

It took her the best part of an hour to dress his wound. She noticed that his whole body, mainly the left side, was covered in graze marks, as if he had been dragged along the ground. She could see that by the next morning he would be a mass of bruises. Every now and again he would mumble some words and at one stage she managed to catch the word: 'Paul'. Then the next time he spoke, he mentioned Smithers and she imagined that he was trying to tell her something, even though it was sub-consciously.

She got up from her kneeling position and went in search of a cigarette. She noticed that her hand was shaking badly when she lit it and that she was hot and flustered. She silently wished that Mr. and Mrs. McClelland had been around to give her some advice. She went upstairs to one of the bedrooms and pulled the blankets off the bed. Quickly she took them back downstairs and spread them over Kane's body. He opened his eyes again and murmured 'Paul . . . Smithers

. . . head . . . organisation . . . '

Elaine looked down at him and then went over to his jacket. She started looking through his pockets. There was nothing in them and she went back to the leather armchair and lifted the blankets and searched through his pockets. She found his wallet and passport in his back pocket. She began to look through them.

Kane woke around ten in the morning. He opened his eyes and stared around the room. He sat up with a jerk when he saw Elaine lying full length on the settee opposite him.

Elaine stirred at the sound of him moving and swung her feet on to the floor. 'Hi, there, Adam, and how are you feeling this morning?'

Kane licked his lips and looked around him. He grimaced at the pain even the moving of his head caused. 'Not too good. Where am I?'

'You're okay here. This is the McClelland's house. You passed out on me last night after I got you here. You've been knocked about quite a bit and I think I know why. I stayed up most of the night and had the radio on. There was a gang killing last night in the same street as where I picked you up. The police said they believed a hand-grenade exploded in the car. Were you mixed up in that in any way?'

Kane nodded his head slowly. He said: 'Yes, it was a friend of mine who was killed. I managed to throw myself out just before it exploded. I landed on the grass verge.'

'Oh, Adam, what have you got yourself into?' asked Elaine, coming over to him and sitting on the arm of the chair. 'I'm so worried about you.'

Kane took his hand from underneath the blankets and placed it on top of hers. 'I'll tell you all about it later, Elaine. I think I'll try and get some more sleep. I still don't feel too good.'

'I'll get you some of my sleeping tablets,' said Elaine, going out of the room.

Kane slept the clock around and woke to the smell of some hot soup being brought into the room. He gently moved his body and found that, although it hurt considerably, he wasn't as stiff as he had been before.

'Hi, it's good to see that you're awake,' said Elaine as she came over to him. 'I thought you'd never wake up.'

Kane smiled up at her.

'Anyway, you must be starving. Look, I've brought you in some hot soup, tomato, and some fresh bread and butter. Do you think you'll be able to manage it on your own?'

Kane nodded his head, and propped himself up by moving one of the pillows down into the small of his back. He took the tray from Elaine and smelt the soup. He suddenly realised that he was starving. He stirred the soup with the spoon and bit a chunk out of the slice of bread. Elaine went to the settee and rested her head in her hands and watched him.

Kane finished the soup and then asked her for a cigarette. She took out two from a cigarette box on the coffee table and lit them with the table lighter. She brought it over to him and put it in his mouth. She sat on the arm of the chair and kissed him on the forehead. She said: 'Well, now that you look as if you're going to survive perhaps you can tell me what's been going on. The newspapers are full of that car explosion.'

Kane thought for a few seconds. He decided that she had a right to know. It wasn't every girl that would take an obviously injured man into her house and nurse him without wanting to know something of the circumstances behind his injury.

'Well, first of all, Elaine, I'm not involved in anything criminal, on my part, that is. I'm an investigator with the West Pacific Insurance Company. I think I mentioned this to you up in Fiji. A few weeks ago I got wind of a swindle which would cost my firm a million dollars. The small details don't matter but I managed to find out quite a bit about this organisation and then, somehow, they got to know that I knew and they tried to have me silenced.'

'Was that up in Fiji?' asked Elaine. 'There was a story going about that two bullets had been found embedded in your bure after you'd left.'

'That was their second try,' said Kane. 'The first was back here in Australia. Once I knew that they were after me, I went and saw my boss and gave him all the facts. That way he would be able to stop this organisation carrying on with the swindle even if I were killed. He advised me to get out of the country for a while until things died down.'

'That was when you came up to Fiji?' asked Elaine.

'That's right. That night, after I left you, I went back to my bure and found the door unlocked. I thought that I must have forgotten to lock it and went in without thinking. Waiting for me was a member of this gang and we had a fight. He had a revolver with a silencer on it and it must have been during the fight that he fired those two shots.'

'Why didn't you report him to the police?' asked Elaine, stubbing out her cigarette in the ashtray.

'I was going to but when I went around to the reception desk I saw the man who had nearly got me in Australia a few days before. That was the first indication I had that it was the same people after me. I thought then, that the best thing for me to do would be to get out of that hotel as quickly as I could. I had no idea how many of the organisation were around. For all I knew there could have been more of them.'

'So that's why you left in a hurry! I was annoyed with you the next morning when you didn't turn up at the beach. Then, when I found out that you'd left the hotel, without even paying your bill I might add, I was really mad! Then I heard this story about the bullet holes in your bure and I didn't know what to think. I got your card a few days later and that cooled me down a bit.'

Kane smiled. He said: 'Believe me, I didn't know whether I was coming or going at that stage. I was stuck in Suva and was trying to get out either on a plane or a boat, but these people were hard on my tail and had the exits watched. Fortunately, I met some people who knew about this yacht which was moored down at the mouth of the Rewa. I made a mad dash down there and managed to get on it.'

'I'm beginning to make sense out of what I know,' said Elaine. 'The next I heard of you was through the newspapers here. There was a report of you being lost overboard from this yacht just outside New Zealand. How was that?'

'Two or three days after we sailed a plane flew over us. It had been hired by these two men from the organisation, and they spotted me sitting on a deckchair on deck. Well, to cut a long story short, they were watching the approaches to Auckland in a powerful motor boat when we arrived. That was when I got into the dinghy and got away.'

'You mean you got into a small dinghy and just rowed away? In the middle of the Pacific?'

'It was either that or be taken aboard the launch and killed.'

'And you managed to make land?' asked Elaine.

'No,' Kane paused as a car roared down the road and then braked suddenly. He cocked his ear as he heard it reversing back up the road. 'A Japanese fishing boat picked me up the next morning. They were inside the twelve mile limit doing some illegal fishing and I made a deal with the captain to be dropped ashore with no questions asked.'

'I think that car has stopped outside the house,' said Elaine. 'I'm not expecting the McClellands back until the day after tomorrow. Never mind, carry on.'

'I was dropped close to a place called Rotorua where these men caught up with me again.'

'They really meant to get you, didn't they?' said Elaine. She got up and parted the curtains and looked out on to the road. She said: 'That car must have gone, there's no sign of it now.'

'That's where I got this bullet through my arm,' said Kane. 'They had me cornered in a place called Hell's Gate. One of them, Ben Collins, fell into a mud pool and while I was getting away a man called Kordina took a shot at me.'

'I think there's someone walking around the house, Adam. Can't you hear something?'

'No,' replied Kane. 'I didn't hear a

thing. I thought I'd lost them but on the plane I bumped into this Kordina fellow who stuck a gun in my ribs and threatened to kill me there and then . . . '

'What, on the plane?' asked Elaine.

'Yes, and he would have done. He was in that state of mind.'

'He must be mad!'

'I'll say! Anyway, I decided to play ball and take my chances once we reached Sydney. We arrived at Kingford-Smith without any trouble and when we were going through Customs I saw Jim Brady waiting for me. I had phoned him from Auckland, but I hadn't made any arrangements with him to meet there. I was going to contact him that night at his office. He noticed that something was wrong and followed us. Kordina was met by another gunman named Hans at the airport and they were going to take me up to The Gap and throw me over. It's a local . . . '

'I know!' said Elaine. 'Mrs. McClelland took me up there the first day I spent here. If they forced you over there you wouldn't have stood a chance!'

'Too right! Jim Brady got into his car and drove towards us. I jumped aside as Jim went by and managed to get into his car. Kordina and Hans then chased us. Hans must have been a terrific driver because he caught up with us. They drew level and then Kordina threw that hand-grenade into Jim's car. I dived out of the door and I thought Jim had gone out his side, but he hadn't and the grenade exploded with him still in it. He didn't have a hope!'

'And that's when you phoned me?' asked Elaine. 'This is where I come into the story. There's one thing though, that I can't work out after all you've told me. How did they know you had gone up to Fiji?'

'That's what puzzled me,' said Kane. 'As far as I was concerned there were only a handful of people who knew where I was going. I thought one of the organisation must have seen me boarding the plane. I can honestly say I didn't know who the informer was until that launch tried to hi-jack me from the yacht. Directly I saw the launch I recognised it and knew at once who the Big Boy was.'

'So you know who this man is?' asked Elaine. 'That should make your Mr. Smithers happy. He sounded perturbed on the phone . . . '

'What the hell do you mean, Elaine! On the phone?' asked Kane, sitting erect in the leather armchair and tightening his grip on Elaine's wrist.

'Why Adam, you're hurting me!' cried Elaine. 'Please let go!'

'When were you talking to Paul Smithers on the phone Elaine? Answer me, it's important!'

'While you were sleeping. You were mumbling in your sleep and I managed to catch a few words. You said 'Paul . . . Smithers . . . ' and something else. I didn't know what you meant but later I searched through your wallet to find out who you were working for. I found a card, that blue one with your name on it, and on the reverse side it gave the address of your head office and Paul Smithers' name. It said that should anything happen to you to phone that number. Why Adam! What have I done wrong!'

'What did you say to Paul?' asked Kane, trying to stand. 'Did you tell him where I was?'

'Yes. I gave him this address.'

'I'll have to get out of here at once!' said Kane. 'You'd better come with me!'

'Why Adam, I don't see . . . '

'Because Paul Smithers happens to be the Big Boy! He happens to be the brains behind the organisation. With me alive and knowing what I do, his whole empire is in jeopardy. All I've got to do is report what I know to the police and he'll be put away for life. Right now, I'm concerned about your safety. You gave him this address and you can bet your bottom dollar that before tonight is out we'll have visitors. Now be a good girl and get your coat and handbag. Don't pack anything, we haven't time.'

Kane's body still ached from the dive from Jim Brady's car but it wasn't enough to stop him from walking about. He picked up his wallet and was about to put it in his back pocket when he heard a loud crack. He stopped and listened. The sound had come from the back of the house and he could still hear Elaine moving around upstairs.

The sound was a familiar one. It was the sound of a lock being forced open. Kane immediately recalled the car which had driven past the house earlier and then braked to a halt and reversed. Elaine had said she had heard someone walking around the house as well. Kane's heart missed a beat as he realised that they were too late. It looked as if the organisation had come for him, and this time there was no way out!

Kane went over to the door and listened. He could hear someone creeping along the hallway. He turned and looked around the room. Beside him, on the side-board, was a heavy brass figurine. He picked it up by the neck and stood behind the door.

A shadow was thrown across the doorway and Kane watched it as it moved closer into the room. He stood on the balls of his feet, ready to pound down the figurine with all his might.

The man stood in the entrance to the room and looked around. Then he

223

cautiously stepped forward. Kane was watching the edge of the door and directly he saw the revolver he brought down the figurine.

But the gunman was ready for such a move and he managed to pull back his arm so that the ornament thudded to the floor without touching him. Then he stepped into the room and turned and faced Kane. He held a snub-nosed .38 at Kane's stomach.

'Well, well, well, if it isn't you again,' said Kordina slowly. 'I don't know how you managed to get away from that car but this time I'm going to finish you off without a question of doubt. You've caused me enough trouble as it is. Where's the girl?'

Kane thought quickly. There was just a chance that she would hear them talking and realise that something was wrong. He answered: 'She's gone out to get a doctor.'

'That's good, although you won't be needing a doctor because you're going to be dead before this minute's up!'

Kane lowered his hands. Somehow, he

managed to tell himself, this was the end for him and he resigned himself to his fate. He looked up at Kordina and spat in has face. He said: 'What are you waiting for, Kordina, or is this the first time you've shot an unarmed man?'

Kordina raised the .38 until it was pointing at Kane's trouser belt. Kane saw the skin on the gunman's knuckles turn white as he began to squeeze the trigger.

15

Element of Surprise

There were two shots, both fired during the same second, as Kane slung himself sideways in a frantic effort to survive the hacking thud of a .38 bullet in his stomach.

Kane hit the carpeted floor and lay still, waiting for the excruciating pain to flow up to his brain. But it didn't come. All that he could feel was a burning sensation on his left hip. Miraculously, he found, he was alive!

There was a second thud and Kane turned his head and saw that Kordina had collapsed beside him. His face had a look of astonishment on it and out of his open mouth came a thin trickle of blood. Kane rolled over and grabbed the revolver which was still clutched in his hand. He got up from the floor slowly and looked around.

Framed in the doorway was Elaine. She had both her hands up to her face and was crying uncontrollably. At her feet, Kane noticed, was a small .22 automatic with an ivory pearl handle.

'Oh, my God!' she cried. 'What have I done? What have I done?'

Kane walked over and put his arm around her shoulder. He led her to the settee. She was crying, her sobs coming in gigantic convulsions from the depths of her body.

'Oh Adam!' she cried, looking up into his eyes. 'I didn't know what to do. I was about to come down the stairs and I happened to look over the landing and saw this man creeping along the hall with this gun in his hand. Light me a cigarette, will you please.'

Kane got up and fetched the cigarette box over. He lit one and then gave it to her. She smoked it for a minute in silence, trying to compose herself. Then she stubbed it out and said: 'After what you told me about these men trying to kill you and seeing that I had told Paul Smithers over the phone where you were and then seeing this man . . . Oh Adam! I was so scared!'

'It's all right now,' said Kane, softly. 'Just sit still, you'll feel better in a few minutes.'

'I knew he was going to kill you, Adam, I could see just by looking at him. He had that look on his face. And then I remembered the automatic I always carry with me. It's only a small gun. My father gave it to me after I was molested one night in New York. I've never fired it before in my life. I didn't know whether it would fire properly, but it was all I could think of. He didn't hear me coming down the stairs, he was talking to you at the time, and I managed to get right up behind him. Then I aimed at the back of his head and pulled the trigger.'

Kane got up from the settee and picked up the automatic. It was an Italian Beretta .22, a harmless gun unless the bullet hit a vital part of the body. Kane moved over and had a look at Kordina and noticed the small hole at the back of his head. Somehow, although she wasn't an expert shot, she had hit him in the one place which would have dropped him like a stone. Kane imagined she must have fired a split second before Kordina had, just long enough for Kordina's hand to drop enough so that the bullet from his gun only grazed the skin of his hip.

He put the Beretta in his coat pocket and then looked at the .38. He found that it was fully loaded except for the one shot which had been fired. He stuck the gun in his trouser belt and went back to Elaine. He sat down beside her.

'Elaine, listen to me for a few seconds,' said Kane, holding her hand in his. 'What you've done tonight is nothing to get upset about. The police won't even bring a charge against you, of that I can assure you. But we will have to inform them of this, if not, it could bring us trouble. I know one of the top Police Inspectors in Sydney and I'll give him a ring later on after we get out of here. At the moment I think we're still in danger. If Kordina came here I should imagine that Hans is also around. He's most probably in the car. I'm going to go outside and have a look.

Do you want to stay here or come with me?'

Elaine got up quickly. She said. 'Don't leave me here with him Adam! Please take me with you!'

He held her hand and then took out the .38. They retraced Kordina's footsteps towards the back of the house. The back door had been forced open and a jemmy lay on the concrete steps outside.

'Stay behind me, Elaine, and keep close to the wall of the house, in the shadows. There's just the chance that Hans might be waiting out the back, in which case I'm going to shoot first and then ask questions.'

They went quietly down the concrete steps and then along the narrow pathway. Kane stopped every few yards and peered into the darkness ready to fire at the slightest hint of a movement. But the garden was quiet and there was no sign of Hans.

They made the cover of a thick hedge which surrounded the property and Kane ducked through the branches and looked out at the road. He looked first to the left and then to the right. There was no sign of a car in either direction. He was just about to pull his head back when a car swung around the corner and came down past the house.

Kane drew in his breath and ducked down, leaving only the top of his head and eyes above the wall. He looked into the car as it drove past and recognised Hans in the driver's seat.

Hans slowed the car down and looked out of the window, then, when there was no sign of Kordina, put his foot on the accelerator and went down the road. He turned left at the next intersection.

Kane pulled himself out of the hedge and faced Elaine. He said: 'Look, Elaine, Hans is driving around the block waiting for Kordina to come out. I've got an idea. You go and get the car and drive it out on to the road, and then take the first turning to the right and park. I'll go back into the house, get your handbag and coat and meet you in the car in a few minutes. But we'll have to hurry and get that car out on the road and out of sight before he completes another circuit. He might start to think that Kordina's taking too much time and decide to do a little investigating of his own. Do you think you could manage that?'

Elaine nodded her head and said: 'I'll do my best but I'm scared as hell!'

'Don't worry, Elaine. I wouldn't ask you to do this if I didn't think you could. I'll be staying around here covering you. Off you go, then.'

Kane watched her as she reversed the car down the drive out on to the road. She engaged the gears and with the tyres squealing in protest, roared off down the road. She took the first turning to the right and Kane heard the engine being cut soon after she was out of sight.

He turned his head and looked up the other way. She had only just made it for a car pulled around the corner and started coming down the road towards him. Kane ducked down out of sight and heard the car pull to a stop outside the gate. It stayed there for several seconds and then moved off again. Kane thought that the next time around Hans would get out and take a look around the house. He

232

hadn't a second to lose.

He started to run down the concrete path but had to slow down to a walk as his aching legs halted him. He climbed the steps and entered the house. He took another look at Kordina and then quickly went upstairs to get Elaine's coat and bag.

He let himself out of the front door, closing it quickly behind him and then ran into the cover of the hedge lining the drive and went down to the gate posts. He looked up and down the road and then started running across to the other side. He was half-way across when he saw the beam of Hans' headlights starting to turn into the road.

Kane ran as fast as he could across the remainder of the road and dived full length over a low wall, just as the beam hit the spot he had been at a second before. He landed in a rose garden, scratching his face on some thorns in the process. He lay still, not daring to move a muscle as the car went by. He heard it stop again and then the car door open. The sounds of Han's feet scraping the gravel on the road came to Kane's ears and then he heard the man spit. After a few seconds pause Hans got back into the car and drove off.

Kane lifted his head and watched the car as it took the next turning to the left. He pulled himself up and stepped back over the wall on to the pavement. He ran along the road and turned the corner. About fifty yards along, parked on the left-hand side of the road, was the car. Kane opened the near-side door and smiled at the sight of Elaine, sprawled across the front seat. He said: 'Good girl. Now let's get out of here!'

Kane turned the next corner and then accelerated down the long, straight road. Ahead was a shopping centre and Kane saw a phone booth on the corner. He stopped the car.

'You can relax now, Elaine,' said Kane. 'I'm going to phone a friend of mine in the police here and have him pick up Hans.'

Kane went into the booth and dialled a number. When he heard the policeman answer he asked for Inspector Davies.

'I'll put you through to his house number right away,' the policeman replied.

After a delay of a few minutes a gruff voice answered the phone and Kane said quickly: 'Mike, this is Adam Kane speaking. Look, I haven't much time but I can put you on to the two men responsible for that car explosion the other night.'

'Can you? Go ahead, Kane.'

'Before I tell you, Mike, I'd like to ask a big favour. Could you try to keep the news out of the papers for a couple of days? That's all I ask. It would help me a hell of a lot if you could.'

'I'll see what I can do on that score,' said the Inspector. 'But I can't make any promises. You know how things are with us.'

'Do your best, Mike. If you send a patrol car to this address,' he gave the house number and the name of the street, 'you'll find a man named Kordina dead in the front lounge. He's been shot by a .22 Beretta in the back of the head. The other man, Hans, I only know his Christian name, will be either outside in a car or prowling around the house. Here's the make of his car and its number.' Kane gave him the details.

'Okay, Kane. Thanks a lot. Where do you fit into all this?'

'I'm mixed up in it right up to my neck,' said Kane. 'Right now I've got to go up to Brisbane to tie up a few loose ends. This should take a couple of days then I'll contact you and put you straight on everything. This fellow Hans will be armed so tell your men not to be heroic.'

'We'll cover ourselves. Where are you speaking from?'

'Look Mike, you'll have to trust me for a couple of days. I'm on to something hot and I've got a good chance of being able to finish it. Just give me a couple of days. Okay?'

The Police Inspector was silent for a few seconds. Then he said: 'Right, Kane, but I'd like a full report as quick as possible.'

Kane put the receiver down and let himself out of the phone booth. 'Well, that's that,' he said to Elaine, as he climbed into the car. 'They'll pick up Hans in a few minutes. Now, do you feel like driving up to Brisbane?'

'Whatever for, Adam?' asked Elaine. 'Can't the police finish this off?'

'No, this is a personal matter.'

'Oh, well, I might as well. Heavens, if I knew all this was going to happen to me I think I would have had second thoughts about falling for you up in Fiji!'

★ ★ ★

'Adam, what do you plan doing once we get to Brisbane?' Elaine asked the question as they were having a cup of coffee in a café at Surfers' Paradise late the following morning. 'You were saying on the way up that you wanted to have it out with Paul Smithers, to find out why he was running this organisation. I've been thinking, why don't you just go to the police and let them pick him up? You could then see him when he's safe and sound in a cell. You might be inviting trouble if you go out to his place to see him.'

Kane shook his head. 'This is how I've worked it out. Paul Smithers must have contacted Kordina and Hans in Sydney after you phoned him. His instructions were to go to the McClelland's house and kill me. Well, we know what happened, but Paul doesn't. As far as he's concerned the assignment went as planned . . . '

'Won't the papers report the killing?'

'I asked the police to see if they could get it shelved for a couple of days. So, provided they do, then Paul Smithers might not realise that I'm on my way up here, maybe I can catch him unawares. I say maybe.'

'Oh Adam, I wish you'd see sense,' said Elaine. 'You've had enough narrow escapes. Why take chances?'

'But this is personal, Elaine. I want to know why he should suddenly turn around and order my death. I think I've got a right to know the answer to that, don't you?'

Elaine was silent. She stared down at her coffee cup, knowing that it would be hopeless to argue any further. Adam Kane, she thought, certainly had a stubborn streak.

They refuelled the car and bought the morning's paper. While Kane drove Elaine scanned the pages for a headline concerning the killing. She looked up after going through the paper twice. She said: 'I can't find anything. It looks as if your police friend has managed to keep it out.'

Kane pulled the car to a stop outside the Berkeley. He switched off the ignition and turned and faced Elaine. He said: 'I have a suite here. I use it on and off throughout the year. We'll go up and you can stay here while I go out and finish off what has to be done. You'll be safe here and nobody will bother you.'

They got out of the car and went up the steps. Kane left Elaine standing at the centre writing table in the foyer and went over to the desk to get his key. They then took the elevator up to his suite.

'What do you want me to do, Adam?' asked Elaine, after Kane had mixed a drink.

'I'd like you to stay here in the suite all afternoon. I'll give you an Inspector's name and phone number before I leave and then tonight I'll phone you and give you the latest news. Then, say half an hour after I've gone to Paul's place, I want you to phone this Inspector and give him Paul's name and address. He'll know what to do from there. This will give me about half an hour with Paul, which is all I'll need. Then the police will arrive and they can do what they like with him.'

'I suppose it's no use arguing with you?' said Elaine. 'You've got your mind made up and nothing will stop you, will it?'

Kane smiled. He said: 'You may think me stubborn, Elaine, but this is the way I've got to handle it.'

Kane finished his drink and cigarette and then left Elaine in the lounge looking through some old *Playboy* magazines, while he went into the bathroom and had a shower and shave.

Half an hour later he emerged feeling more relaxed than he had since boarding the jet in Auckland.

'I'm off now, Elaine,' he said, bending over and kissing her cheek. 'Don't leave this room unless you have to. I'll give you a ring just before I go, giving you Paul's address and then you can call this number half an hour later and give the person who answers the information.' He gave her a slip of paper with the Inspector's phone number on it.

Elaine put down the magazine and forced a smile. She said: 'I'll stay here, Adam, and do as you say but I won't be happy until you come back here in one piece. I'll be worried stiff!'

Kane said: 'Surprise should be on my side, Elaine, and that's half the battle.'

Elaine got up hurriedly from the settee. She put both her arms around Kane's neck and kissed him on the mouth. Then she said softly into his ear: 'Hurry back, you mad fool.'

Kane turned and walked towards the door, stopping on the way to pick up the .38 revolver which he had taken off Kordina. Then, with another look at Elaine and a wave of his hand, he let himself out of the suite.

Kane got into McClelland's car and started the engine. He sat back in the seat with both hands resting on the steering wheel. He drew in his breath and then let it out slowly. He said to himself: 'Well, kiddo, this could be it.' He let out the clutch and headed for the police station.

★   ★   ★

'Inspector Barton won't be long,' said the constable, showing him into an office. 'Take a seat for a while.'

'Thanks,' said Kane.

Minutes later the office door opened and Inspector Ken Barton came in. He looked at Kane. 'What the hell have you been doing? You're wanted in New Zealand for questioning . . .'

'What would you say if I gave you the Big Boy on a plate?' interrupted Kane.

'The Big Boy!' exclaimed the Inspector, taken aback. 'You know who he is?'

Kane nodded his head. He said: 'That's right. I know who he is and I know what he does as a cover job. You remember that last time I was here, when I was attacked by that hitch hiker? Well, that was the start of things. Sit down and I'll give you the whole story, but first of all, I want you to promise me that you'll let me finish this my way, that you'll let me leave here after what I've told you. In return you'll be contacted here later on tonight with his name, address and anything else you want to know. Is that a deal?'

'You've got me over a barrel, haven't you? You always did work in unorthodox ways but this time I'll have to play ball. We've been after this bloke for years and we haven't even cracked the ice. Let's hear what you've got to say.'

Kane began at the beginning, from the time when Danny Hurst first contacted him and told him about the swindle involving the Melbourne Cup. He explained Danny's strange death, the correct story behind the hitch hiker, his sudden departure to Fiji and everything that had happened to him up there, his flight to New Zealand and then back to Sydney.

' . . . friend of mine met me in Sydney,' Kane concluded. 'You'll know the name, Jim Brady. We managed to get away from these two hired guns but they chased us through the streets, finally catching us up and throwing . . . '

' . . . a hand-grenade into the car?' asked the Inspector. 'So, you were mixed up in that, were you? You've really been around during the last few weeks. We had a report about a killing down in Sydney, the name sounds familiar, Kordina. Does this tie up with what you've told me?'

'Yes,' answered Kane. 'The gunman who caught me on the plane, the one that threw the hand-grenade and the one that was found dead in Sydney are all the same person. I was a witness to Kordina's death and I informed Inspector Davies, of Sydney, about it. You don't know whether they picked up the other gunman, do you?'

'Yes, they picked him up all right. It was in the report. It's funny, your name wasn't mentioned in it, how was that?'

'Maybe because I asked Davies to hold off until I had seen this thing through.'

Inspector Barton looked out of the window and watched the scene below. Then he turned and said: 'By rights, Kane, I should make a report out straight away to my superior. This is something big. But I'll play ball with you, on one condition: don't let anything go wrong. I'll be out on my ear without a pension if it does! Tell you what, I'll give you a time limit. If I don't hear from you by twelve tonight I'll go in by myself. I've got a pretty good idea who the Big Boy is from what you've told me. What do you say?'

'That would suit me fine,' answered Kane. 'When I leave here I've got one or two things to do then I'm going out to see this Big Boy. While I'm going out there, though, you'll be contacted and given his name and address, so if anything was to happen to me you'd still be able to get the man. All you have to do is come out to this address with some of your boys and pick him up. All I'll want is about half an hour. That's all.'

The Inspector looked at Kane. He said: 'Listen, Kane. Don't let this go to your head. From what you've told me you've had some close scrapes with this gang. If this Big Boy knows he's cornered he might try and have it out with you. Is there anything you want?'

Kane thought for a few seconds, then he said: 'There is one thing you might let me have. I remember reading about a year ago of a mad dog that held a family hostage. They called you fellows in and you went to the house with a special rifle which fired doped darts. The dog keeled over in about ten seconds after it was hit. Do you have one of those rifles around?'

'Yes, they're standard equipment around here now. I could loan you one, unofficially, if you want it.'

'That would be great,' said Kane. 'And about half a dozen darts.'

'Sounds like you're going to find your man in the centre of the lion's cage at the zoo,' said the Inspector. 'Okay, I'll get you one. Hold on here for a while.'

The Inspector left the room and Kane lit another cigarette. He thought that everything was working out fine. The police were playing ball with him, more so than he had expected. But, he thought, that's how it should be. There had been other times when he had helped them out, helped them out of quite a few tight corners. They could afford just this once to let him have a little leeway. The net result would be a big feather in the

Inspector's hat. The Big Boy on a plate had been the aim of the majority of policemen for the past two years.

Inspector Barton came back carrying a .22 rifle. He handed it over to Kane and also a small box containing six darts.

'Directly that stuff gets into the animal's bloodstream,' he said, 'it starts working. If it's a dog, it'll be out like a light inside ten seconds. The bigger the animal, the longer it takes.'

'Thanks, Ken,' said Kane, holding out his hand. 'You'll be hearing from a contact of mine later tonight. Stay around until then. It might be advisable to come armed to this address. Anything could happen.'

'We'll look after ourselves, don't you worry,' replied the Inspector. 'I only hope to hell things don't go wrong and you let this Big Boy get away. There could be fireworks if my boss ever got to hear of how I've handled this.'

'You'll be right,' said Kane, opening the door to the office.

He walked out of the police station and placed the rifle on the back seat of the car. He put the box of darts in the glove compartment next to the revolver. He looked at his watch and saw that it was nearly five. He started up the engine.

Kane drove up town and parked the car opposite the front entrance to the West Pacific Insurance Company building. He relaxed and lit a cigarette and watched the swing doors, waiting for the day staff to leave.

He didn't have long to wait. Soon the doors were flung wide open by the night porter and the day staff started streaming out on to the wide, sunlit pavement. He recognised quite a few of the employees as they came through the doors and he wondered just how many of them were mixed up in the organisation.

The number of employees slowly dwindled until the pavement was clear. Kane thought he'd wait for another ten minutes before he ventured into the building.

Kane smoked one more cigarette and then decided it was time to make a move. He got out of the car, locked the doors and then crossed the road. He walked quickly up the steps and entered the elevator.

His office door opened softly and Kane quickly entered. He glanced around. Everything looked as if it were in the same place as when he had left.

He crossed to his desk and sat down. He began opening the drawers one by one and studying the contents. When he got to the bottom one he knew for sure that his desk had been opened. He remembered distinctly leaving a red file on the top, yet now a yellow one was in its place. Kane imagined that someone had been through it to see if there was any incriminating evidence left around.

Kane crossed the office and opened the door. He glanced up and down the corridor. He made his way towards a door marked 'Records'.

'Records' was a large room full of filing cabinets. It was here that a copy of each policy was kept. Kane took the keys out of his pocket and went across to the filing cabinet marked: 'CH'. He opened it and looked through for the Cheyney file.

He found it and pulled it out. There

were several policies and Kane took each
one out separately and studied them. The
fifth one he came to was the one he
wanted. He took it out and then went
over to one of the windows and read it,
holding it against the fading light. He saw
that it hadn't been cancelled. The
authorising signature on the policy was
that of Paul Smithers.

Kane folded the policy up and put it
inside his coat pocket. He returned the
file back into the drawer then closed the
cabinet, locking it at the same time. He
walked quickly back down the corridor to
his office.

He let himself in and locked the door.
He switched on the light and pulled down
the green shade to cover the glass
partition. He walked over to the desk and
sat down, taking out the policy and
flattening it on the top of the desk. He
took out some notepaper and his pen and
then stared up at the ceiling. He
wondered how he should start the letter,
the letter which would tell all about Paul
Smithers and the organisation; the letter
which he planned mailing before he went

to see Paul Smithers that night just in case something went wrong.

He took up his pen and started writing.

At half past seven he finished and sat back in his chair and read it through. He folded the letter after signing it and then enclosed the policy. He took out a long envelope from his drawer and addressed it to Inspector Ken Barton. He searched around for a stamp and then stuck it on the top right-hand corner. He thought that the letter, now that it had been written, was a load off his mind.

Kane looked out of the window and saw that it was almost dark. He decided that it was time he started moving. He picked up the phone and dialled the number of the Berkeley.

The switchboard operator answered and he asked to be put through to his suite. He heard the call being connected and then heard Elaine's voice on the other end.

'Adam here,' he said. 'How did you spend the afternoon?'

'Worrying about you, Adam,' Elaine replied. 'Where are you?'

'I'm at the office. I'm just about to leave. Look, Elaine, it's nearly over now. This is the last phase. I've just checked with 'Records' here and the policy hasn't been cancelled.'

'So the bet is still on?'

'Yes, it's still on and there's two days to go to the deadline. I should imagine that all the bets are pouring into Cheyney's right now. Here's what I'd like you to do. It's now five minutes past eight. At exactly a quarter to nine I want you to phone Inspector Barton. I gave you his number earlier. Tell him you're ringing on my behalf and tell him the name and address he has been waiting for is this. Have you got a pencil and paper handy?'

'Yes, Adam.'

'Good girl. Now the name, of course, is Paul Smithers. The address is: The Grange, out on the main road north. He knows what to do from there. I've had a long talk with him this afternoon.'

'I guess there's no chance of my being able to talk you out of making this visit tonight? Somehow I feel as if something's going to go wrong,' said Elaine.

'Don't worry, Elaine,' said Kane. 'I've covered my tracks as much as possible and the police will arrive before I've been there very long. I've got the element of surprise on my side. Don't forget to phone at a quarter to nine. I'll be back with you as soon as I can.'

He hung up the phone and was about to pick up the letter when there was a knock on the door.

'Hell,' said Kane to himself.

He put the letter in his inside coat pocket and walked across the office and unlocked the door. He opened it wide.

'Hello, Mr. Kane,' said the night porter. 'I saw the light on in your office from under the door and I said to myself, now, I wonder who that can be? Well, well, well, and how are you?'

'I'm fine, Albert,' replied Kane. 'Just come in to check a few things. I'm off again right away.'

'It's good to see you again, Mr. Kane. The office hasn't been the same since you left for Fiji. I've noticed one or two of the young ladies walking around with long faces. They'll be pleased to hear you're back.'

'That remains to be seen,' said Kane with a smile. 'You must excuse me, Albert, but I've got to go. I've got an important appointment tonight.'

Kane switched off the light and closed the door and then walked quickly along the corridor to the elevators. He pressed the button and the doors opened immediately.

Albert stood in the corridor watching him leave. After the elevator doors had closed he went into Kane's office and picked up the phone. He dialled Paul Smithers' home number. He waited for him to answer.

16

The Trump Card

Kane stopped the car about two hundred yards past the main gates to Paul Smithers' house. He pulled the car on to the verge and switched off the engine.

He took out the revolver from the glove compartment and checked it. Satisfied, he tucked it into his trouser band.

Then he leant over to the back seat and picked up the rifle. He studied the reloading system. The rifle was powered by a CO_2 cartridge which was screwed into the stock and Kane judged that it would have an accurate range of about twenty-five yards. He took out the darts and tried his hand at reloading. After six tries he had it down pat, but there was going to be at least seven or eight seconds when he would be vulnerable.

It was the dogs that had Kane worried most. There were two ways into the grounds, one was to drive in and up to the front door, but that way would lose the element of surprise. The other was to climb the wall and try to evade the dogs or knock them out. Kane knew that the element of surprise was what mattered most.

He looked at his watch and saw that it was twenty past eight. He had about half an hour before the police came. He threw out his cigarette and climbed out of the car.

The moon was waning but now and again it came out from behind a blanket of clouds and he could see quite far in the eerie half light. He pushed his way through the undergrowth and came to the ten foot high brick wall which surrounded the grounds. He started climbing.

Ahead of him he could make out the outline of the house. There weren't any lights showing and Kane had a feeling that he might be too late; that Paul Smithers might have read the writing on the wall and had already cleared out.

But just then, as he was studying the ground before him, he saw a light flicker and then heard the baying of the dogs. A door opened for a brief second and he caught sight of a person silhouetted against the open door. Then the door closed again and all that he could hear was the drumming as the two huge Ridgebacks roamed the grounds.

He walked towards the house, stopping every few yards and crouching down on his knees to look for the dogs. He wondered what he would do if they came for him at the same time. He felt to make sure that the revolver was still in place. The thought of being torn to pieces by their gleaming wet jaws caused a shiver of fear to run up his spine.

And then he saw one. It came towards him with its head down, running in a loping motion. Kane brought the rifle up to his shoulder and waited for the dog to come into range.

It was a hideous sight. The dog's jaws were open and it was baying, calling its mate to the prey. There was a glint in its eyes which turned Kane's legs to rubber.

He waited until the dog was about fifteen yards away and then pressed the trigger. He felt the rush of air and heard the massive dog yelp as the dart entered its shoulder. But the dog's stride didn't break and he bore down on to Kane with all his might.

Kane jumped to his feet and swiped at the dog's head with the butt of the rifle. He managed to contact and the dog faltered for one brief second. Then it prepared itself for the death blow. It crouched ready to spring up at Kane's neck, with its jaws wide open. Kane ran backwards using the rifle as a club, ready to strike out if it sprang forward.

Then the drug started to work. The dog took a step forward, faltered, and then keeled over on to its side with two of its legs sticking up in the air. It was out cold!

Kane swallowed the saliva which had forced itself into his mouth and started to reload. He pulled out a dart from his pocket and tried to find the hole but found his hand was shaking so much that he dropped it on to the grass. He cursed to himself and pulled out another one.

Kane waited for several seconds, searching furtively for the second dog which he knew must be around. Then, when it hadn't appeared, he ventured towards the house. Ahead of him was a group of bushes and he started to make for them.

He took a couple of steps and then stopped in his tracks. He dropped to his knees and stared at the bushes. He saw a slight movement and could just make out the hind quarters of the other dog standing half in and half out of the shadows.

He lifted the rifle up to his shoulder and aimed at the hind quarters. Gently he squeezed the trigger.

He fired at the same time as the dog jumped forward and the dart missed and thudded through the bushes. The Ridgeback broke cover and came at Kane.

Kane swore and got to his feet. He knew that he wouldn't have time to reload; it was going to be him against the dog.

The Ridgeback jumped from four yards away and Kane raised his left arm up to his face as protection against the flashing feet and snapping jaws. With his right hand he thrust forward with all his might, striving to force the barrel of the rifle into the dog's eye. The barrel missed the dog's eye but went into its open mouth.

Kane saw what had happened and he brought down his left hand to grip the rifle's stock. The barrel went right to the back of the dog's mouth and a weird choking sound came from its throat. The force of the dog's charge threw Kane to the ground but he still kept hold of the rifle, pushing with all his strength in an effort to pierce a vital part of the dog's inside. A paw flailed at his chest and he felt a searing pain as the claws ripped through his clothes.

The Ridgeback choked on the rifle barrel and Kane twisted his body so that he could get out from under the heavy weight. As he struggled to his feet, still holding the rifle with his left hand, he pulled out the revolver with his right and gripped it by the barrel. He brought it down hard on the Ridgeback's skull, with a sickening thud.

There was a crack and the dog dropped like a stone. Kane got to his feet and stared down at the lifeless form. He could see at a glance that the dog was dead, the heavy butt of the revolver had cracked its skull wide open.

Kane let go of the rifle and stumbled off into the bushes. His knees felt as though they were going to collapse on him and he felt sick to the stomach. He held on to the trunk of a tree.

Minutes later he lit a cigarette, shielding the flame of the match from the house by cupping his hand around it. He drew the smoke down into his lungs in an effort to calm his nerves. The fight with the Ridgebacks had sapped a lot of strength out of his body.

He threw the cigarette away and looked up at the house. As he watched a light was switched on in one of the bedrooms.

He climbed the steps up to the front door and slowly turned the handle. The handle twisted for half a turn and then stopped. The door was locked. Kane looked at the side windows and saw that one of them was half open, on the latch.

He stuck the revolver back into his belt and put his hand in the opening and unhooked the window. He pulled it open, stopping when the frame creaked on the woodwork.

When he had it open wide enough he climbed through. He sat on the ledge staring into the hallway, waiting for his eyes to become accustomed to the darkness. He listened for any sounds, but the house was quiet.

Kane slowly let himself off the ledge and stood on the rug. He could make out a flickering light coming from underneath the door which led into Paul's study.

Kane moved over to the door and pressed his ear to it. There was no other sound but the fire. He twisted the handle and slowly opened it. He walked into the room, closed the door and looked around.

Then, suddenly, in a blinding flash, the lights were switched on.

Kane went for the revolver in his trouser band but Paul Smithers, who was seated behind the desk with a double-barreled 12 gauge shotgun in his hands said to him: 'I wouldn't if I were you, Kane. I could blow your head off before you got half way to it.'

Kane turned and faced him. He said: 'So you were expecting me?'

Paul got up and came around the desk. He still held the shotgun at the ready and he had his finger on the trigger. He said: 'Yes, I've been expecting you for quite a while. The night porter phoned me a while back. I guessed that your next port of call would be here. Tell me, how did you get past the dogs? I could hear them going after somebody in the grounds but I didn't hear any shots. I thought maybe they had got you.'

'I came prepared for them,' said Kane. 'And even if they had got me it would have been too late. Your game's up, Paul. Whatever happens to me the authorities will still know that you are the Big Boy. I've posted a letter tonight to the police telling them the whole story. Whatever you do now, Paul, will be to no avail, so you might as well put down that shotgun and give yourself up.'

'Not a hope, Kane. I've got too much to lose. Besides, don't you think I've planned for this day? Don't you think I've always envisaged this happening? You can't play with fire, like I've been doing and not expect to get burnt. Sure, you've beaten me. As far as Australia is concerned and the Company, I'm finished. But there's plenty of other places in the world where a man can live, especially a rich man with hard cash.'

'So you think you can get out of this?' asked Kane, glancing at the clock above the fireplace and seeing that it was coming up to a quarter to nine. 'Your plan, whatever it is, would have failed had I brought the police with me,' said Kane. 'How about that?'

'I know you better than most,' replied Paul. 'I knew you'd come up here by yourself. You have an inquisitive nature, Kane, and you always like to finish off a case by yourself, without any outside help. Just check your record and you'll see that your work falls into a pattern, like a criminal's *modus operandi*. I can read you like a book.'

'That was a hell of a risk to take,' said Kane. 'I could have changed my methods.'

'But you didn't. My guess is that you've asked the police to come up here later on, after you've had a talk with me. I can see that I'm right by the way you keep looking over at the clock. But they won't get me. Directly I received the phone call from the night porter I put into effect my escape plan. Kathreen's upstairs now putting a few things into an overnight bag. While I've been waiting for you I've been burning all of my private papers referring to the organisation.' He picked up a black notebook from off the desk and held it up. 'That's all that remains of the organisation I built up. In this book is the name and address of every member. It will go with me. You or the police won't find anything else in the house or at the office that will incriminate anyone.'

Kane walked slowly over to the desk. Paul Smithers watched him, holding the shotgun so that it was always pointing at his feet. Paul Smithers said: 'Take out that gun from your waistband, Kane, and lay it on the desk. Don't try anything funny when you take it out, either, you wouldn't stand a chance against this.'

Kane took the revolver out of his belt. He laid it on top of the desk and then looked at Paul. He asked: 'And what are you going to do with me, Paul? Are you going to finish off what your henchmen couldn't do?'

'No, Kane. I don't think I could kill you, not in cold blood. The dogs were another thing altogether. If they got you I wouldn't feel as if the blood was on my hands. It's a curious thing that, the feeling of guilt.'

Kane moved away from the desk and took out his cigarettes from his coat pocket. He took his time. He was wondering how he could keep him talking. Even now, with the clock showing fourteen minutes to nine, Paul Smithers would have to have a quick method of escape.

Kane shrugged his shoulders. He said: 'Paul, there's been one thing on my mind since I found out that you were the Big Boy. How come you ended up like this? How come you turned to running a criminal organisation when you were already on top of the world? Was it money?'

Paul Smithers went back to the desk and sat down. He laid the shotgun on top of the desk and took the revolver and placed it in one of the side drawers. He replied: 'No, it wasn't money, Kane. I have more than enough. Maybe I've always had a little larceny in me, how else could I have got to the top? You've got to be brutal and a bit dishonest to get anywhere these days. It's only by taking risks that lesser men won't that you get anywhere in this world. I did just that, ever since I started with the Company. I played one against the other and watched them fall by the wayside, then stepped in and took their place. It was all really a game, one big game, and once I got to the top, got the power I wanted, life turned dull. There wasn't any of the old excitement left. My mind had to turn to bigger things.'

'And where does Kathreen, your wife, come into this?'

'Ah, Kathreen,' said Paul. 'Now there's a woman for you! She was like me, always the best and knew how to get it. That's why I married her. She was behind me in every way. Sometimes she was the one who suggested things we ought to do, swindles which, with some real planning, could be achieved. She thought out this Melbourne Cup job. She was on to it the same day that I mentioned to her about Cheyney's wanting us to cover the policy. She worked out the odds and it looked so simple . . . '

The door of the study opened and Kane turned around. Paul's wife, Kathreen, came into the room. She was carrying two small suitcases. 'Are you ready, Paul? I can hear Peters coming,' she said, completely ignoring Kane.

'Yes, my dear. All is ready.' Paul Smithers turned to Kane and said: 'So it looks like we've won in the end, Kane. It's rather sad leaving this place and this country, but there you are, you can't have everything however much you try. My escape plan is so well worked out that it will take the authorities months to find out. That noise you can hear,' he stopped speaking and cocked his ear, the sound of a loud, slow-turning engine came into the study, 'that's my trump card. A helicopter! It has a range of well over two hundred miles and at the end will be my own personal plane to take us to our next destination and from there . . . well, I'll leave that for the authorities to find out. I've got money in practically every bank of importance throughout the world. Our future is assured.'

Kathreen moved over to the french windows and threw them open. The cool night air swirled into the study and the remains of the burnt papers in the fireplace burst into flames. Kane looked beyond Paul Smithers and his wife and saw the helicopter landing on the lawn. The revolving blades twinkled in the reflection from the lights of the study.

Kane glanced back at the clock above the fireplace and saw that it was almost nine. At any moment the police would be arriving.

'Take the two suitcases and go over to Peters,' said Paul to his wife. 'Tell him I'll be over in a few seconds.'

Kathreen went out of the french doors.

She stopped and turned on the top step. She asked: 'And how about him, Paul? Are you going to let him get away with this?'

'Hurry along, Kathreen,' replied Paul. 'I'll look after this end.'

Kane watched as Kathreen walked towards the helicopter. He saw her approach from the rear, keeping well out of the way of the swirling blades. She handed the suitcases to the pilot and then climbed up into the cockpit.

Paul Smithers turned to Kane. He said: 'This is where we part, Kane, I suppose you think I'm going to blast you to Kingdom Come, but you're going to be surprised. I've always had a soft spot for you. It was a pity you were such a good investigator. If you hadn't have been you would never have picked up the threads of this scheme of ours and all this, Hurst's death, the attempts on your life, my having to leave behind all I've built up, would never have come about. But there you are,' he shrugged his shoulders. 'I have no regrets, not even about hiring someone to kill you. You were in my way

270

and anyone who gets in my way has to go. That is the law in my particular jungle.'

'I feel sorry for you, Paul,' said Kane. 'You're not the same Paul Smithers I used to know. Something's happened to you over the years, something which I can't understand. In my estimation you haven't reached the top, you've gone to the bottom of humanity.'

Paul Smithers brought the shotgun up and stared at Kane. There were beads of perspiration forming on his temples. 'You shouldn't have said that!' he shouted.

A shaft of light swung into the room and Kane glanced quickly over Paul's shoulder. He saw that a car had just turned into the driveway. It looked as if Ken Barton was going to turn up at the right moment.

Paul Smithers noticed the headlights and turned his head. Kane made his final move. He jumped forward and grabbed hold of the long barrel of the shotgun, turning it away from his body directly he caught hold of the cold metal.

But Paul Smithers wasn't caught off guard and he wrenched the shotgun away.

Kane was overbalanced and stumbled forward against the desk.

To kill a man in cold blood is one thing, but to give an order for another to kill the same man is entirely different. So it was with Paul Smithers. He had the chance to blast Kane with both barrels but he didn't have the nerve, the guts, to pull the triggers. Instead he brought the stock of the gun around and brought it down on Kane's head.

The blow stunned Kane and he fell against the wooden legs of the desk. His head hurt and his eyes stung from the force of the blow. He tried to raise himself on his elbows but found he couldn't support his weight. Above him he could hear Paul Smithers picking up the black notebook off the desk and putting it in his pocket. Then there was the sound of the shotgun being thrown on to the leather chair and the sounds of his footsteps going down the concrete steps to the lawn.

Kane shook his head again and grasped hold of the top of the desk. He managed to pull himself up. The room started to spin around. He took a deep breath. The glare from the headlights of the approaching car shone into the study and he suddenly became aware of shouting above the sound of the helicopter's engine.

Kane looked out across the lawn. Paul Smithers was running the last ten yards to the helicopter. He glanced quickly over his shoulder, in the direction of the car and then headed straight for the cockpit.

Kane could see what was going to happen a split second before the whirling blade thudded into Paul's shoulder. The force of the blow lifted him clean off the ground and flung him five yards across the lawn. His body landed in a crumpled heap of broken bones and bloody flesh.

Then the tension of the evening caught up with Kane; the fight with the two Ridgebacks, the blow on the head, the accumulation of the last few weeks and he felt a black wave of unconsciousness pass gradually up his body. Just before he passed out he imagined he heard Elaine's voice crying: 'Adam, Adam! Are you all right?'

He hit the floor with a thud.

17

Something to Talk About

Elaine poured out a healthy slug of brandy and brought it over to where Kane was lying and cupped his head in her lap. She held the glass to his lips and gently tipped the amber liquid into his mouth.

Kane unconsciously swallowed the brandy and then coughed. He opened his eyes and tried to sit up. Elaine said softly: 'It's all over with now, Adam. Just lie there and relax.'

Kane looked around the study. Then he said: 'Did Kathreen get away?'

'Yes,' replied Elaine. 'The helicopter rose up in the air just as we were climbing out of the car. We all saw that man run into the blades. It was a horrible sight! I suppose that was Paul Smithers?'

Kane nodded his head. He said: 'He

made his last mistake. What's happening outside?'

'I don't know,' replied Elaine. 'Directly we arrived here all the policemen jumped out of the car and rushed over to the man on the ground. The Inspector told me to stay in the car but I was afraid something had happened to you and I dashed up here. I found you lying here with a terrific bump on your forehead. I thought for a second that you had been killed. There was a shotgun on the seat beside you.'

Kane forced a smile. He said: 'I nearly bought it with Paul, I provoked him too much. I knew that the police were on the way and I was trying to keep him talking. I found out quite a bit about him. It's all rather sick. He was power crazy.'

Footsteps scraped on the concrete steps leading into the study and Kane turned his head to see who it was. Ken Barton came into the room, followed by two constables. He was holding the black notebook in his hand. He looked towards Kane and then said: 'Well Kane, and how do you feel?'

Kane shrugged his shoulders. He said:

'Not too bad, considering. Nothing that a week's sleep won't cure.'

'You'll be able to have that when we've got all these odds and ends tied up. First of all, I think you were crazy to try what you did. There'd have been hell to pay if something had gone wrong. Even now I think I'll have a hard time talking my way out of how this was handled to my superiors.'

'But look what you've got,' said Kane, indicating the black notebook. 'You'll be able to get the whole organisation with the information in that book.'

'That's one consolation. This book will save us a lot of work.' He scratched his head. 'Now,' he continued, 'I think we had all better go down to the station and get this down on paper while it's fresh in our minds. Also, I hope you'll be able to give us some information about a certain car explosion in Sydney the other night and a statement concerning the body of a man found in a suburban house. I've been pestered all afternoon by the Sydney office. Your name's mud as far as they're concerned. Do you feel up to it?'

Kane got up. He held Elaine's hand and started walking towards the open windows. He said: 'The sooner the better. Let's go.'

★   ★   ★

It was ten in the morning when the police car dropped Elaine and Kane at the entrance to the Berkeley. The sun was burning and a faint wind was blowing off the river. It was going to be a perfect day.

The elevator took them up and Elaine produced the door key out of a pocket in her dress. She unlocked the door and led the way in. She said: 'Here we are, safe and sound. Now, Adam, you go and sit down while I get you a drink. I'll have some breakfast sent up.'

'A stiff drink and a cup of black coffee would be fine,' said Kane, making his way over to the settee. 'Hell, am I glad that's all over with! I wonder if they've found where the helicopter landed?'

'The Inspector said they'd be on to it before tonight. What do you think will happen to Kathreen?'

'I don't know,' replied Kane, putting his legs up and placing a cushion underneath his head. 'I don't know and right now, I don't care.' He closed his eyes.

Elaine poured out two drinks and then went over to the phone to order the coffee. She returned to the room to find Kane almost asleep. She sat down beside him and kissed him on the lips. She said: 'You're crazy, Adam, but I'm falling for you. You're the most exciting man I've ever known.'

Kane opened his eyes for a brief second and looked up at her. He said: 'Stay around, Elaine. Stay around and in a few days' time I'll really show you around this country. I'll make up for all of this.'

'I'll be here,' said Elaine. 'I'll be here for always if you want me to be.'

'Now that sounds like an interesting matter to discuss. But later, Elaine. Later.'

'Yes, Adam,' she said, kissing him again. 'We'll talk about it later.'

We do hope that you have enjoyed reading this large print book.

Did you know that all of our titles are available for purchase?

We publish a wide range of high quality large print books including:
Romances, Mysteries, Classics
General Fiction
Non Fiction and Westerns

Special interest titles available in large print are:
The Little Oxford Dictionary
Music Book, Song Book
Hymn Book, Service Book

Also available from us courtesy of Oxford University Press:
Young Readers' Dictionary
(large print edition)
Young Readers' Thesaurus
(large print edition)

For further information or a free brochure, please contact us at:
Ulverscroft Large Print Books Ltd.,
The Green, Bradgate Road, Anstey,
Leicester, LE7 7FU, England.
Tel: (00 44) **0116 236 4325**
Fax: (00 44) **0116 234 0205**

Other titles in the
Linford Mystery Library:

DEATH OF A
LOW HANDICAP MAN

Brian Ball

When Tom Tyzack is viciously beaten to death with a golf club on the local golf course, PC Arthur Root, the local village bobby, is in the unenviable position of having to question his fellow club members. He is regarded with scorn by the detective in charge of the case, and the latter's ill-natured attitude toward the suspects does little to assist him in solving the mystery. But it is Root who, after a second brutal murder, stumbles on the clue that leads to the discovery of the murderer's identity.

ONE SWORD LESS

Colin D. Peel

Working on a defence project in a Research Laboratory, electronic engineer Richard Brendon discovers that he has become part of the cold war. Agonisingly, Brendon is required to balance the lives of his wife and children against co-operation with a foreign power. Forced to use his technical expertise to further a plan to precipitate nuclear war, he takes desperate action to prevent the project and save millions of people from certain destruction.

POSTMAN'S KNOCK

J. F. Straker

Inspector Pitt has a problem. The postman in Grange Road has mysteriously vanished. Had he absconded with the mail — been kidnapped or perhaps murdered? And why had he delivered only some of the letters? The people of Grange Road seem averse to police inquiries. Was there a conspiracy to remove the postman? Before any questions are answered assault, blackmail and sudden death disturb the normal peace of Grange Road.